**Also by Carole Maso**

Ghost Dance
The Art Lover
AVA

# THE AMERICAN WOMAN
# IN THE CHINESE HAT

*a novel*

## Carole Maso

A PLUME BOOK

PLUME

Published by the Penguin Group
Penguin Books USA Inc., 375 Hudson Street,
New York, New York 10014, U.S.A.
Penguin Books Ltd, 27 Wrights Lane, London W8 5TZ, England
Penguin Books Australia Ltd, Ringwood, Victoria, Australia
Penguin Books Canada Ltd, 10 Alcorn Avenue,
Toronto, Ontario, Canada M4V 3B2
Penguin Books (N.Z.) Ltd, 182–190 Wairau Road,
Auckland 10, New Zealand

Penguin Books Ltd, Registered Offices:
Harmondsworth, Middlesex, England

Published by Plume, an imprint of Dutton Signet,
a division of Penguin Books USA Inc.
This is an authorized reprint of a hardcover edition published by
Dalkey Archive Press. For information address: Dalkey Archive Press,
4241 Illinois State University, Normal, IL 61790-4241.

First Plume Printing, October, 1995
10  9  8  7  6  5  4  3  2  1

This book was written at the Michael Karolyi Foundation in Vence,
France, with the added support of a literature grant from the National
Endowment for the Arts.

Portions of this novel first appeared, in somewhat different form, in
*Conjunctions, George Washington Review, The Journal, Ploughshares,
Shankpainter, Yellow Silk,* and in *Slow Hand: Women Writing Erotica,* edited
by Michele Slung (Harper Collins, 1992).

Excerpt from "Ash Wednesday" in *Collected Poems 1909–1962* by T. S.
Eliot, copyright 1936 by Harcourt Brace & Company, copyright © 1964,
1963 by T. S. Eliot, reprinted by permission of the publisher. "Sunday
Morning" and "Mere Being" from *The Palm at the Mind of Mind, Selected
Poems and a Play* by Wallace Stevens reprinted with permission of Alfred
A. Knopf, Inc. Excerpt from "The Young Prince and the Princess" by John
Ashbery from *Contemporary American Poetry* (Penguin UK, 1962) is used
with the permission of Georges Borchardt, Inc. for the author. Copyright
© 1962 by John Ashbery.

*(The following page constitutes an extension of this copyright page.)*

Partially funded by grants from the National Endowment for the Arts and the Illinois Arts Council.

Ⓟ REGISTERED TRADEMARK—MARCA REGISTRADA

ISBN: 0-452-27507-5 CIP Data is available.

Printed in the United States of America

PUBLISHER'S NOTE
This is a work of fiction. Names, characters, places, and incidents either are the products of the author's imagination or are used fictitiously, and any resemblance to actual persons, living or dead, events, or locales is entirely coincidental.

BOOKS ARE AVAILABLE AT QUANTITY DISCOUNTS WHEN USED TO PROMOTE PRODUCTS OR SERVICES. FOR INFORMATION PLEASE WRITE TO PREMIUM MARKETING DIVISION, PENGUIN BOOKS USA INC., 375 HUDSON STREET, NEW YORK, NEW YORK 10014.

In the book it will say that he loved France most. That he was
intelligent and he did not know it. That he was beautiful.
Pour Stéphane, avec tendresse.

For Helen.
In the book it will say forever.

And for Catherine and Lucien, l'innocence des fleurs,
for their company.

# Part One

# 1

Everyone here is kissing everyone on the cheeks—once,
twice, three times—this summer, one of the hottest in years,
I'm told, on La Côte d'Azur, where I have come to write. But
I'm not kissing anyone; I'm waiting for her.

She has written to me: "How much I miss you! Beneath all
I do is an undercurrent of sadness at your absence. I think of
you without knowing I am thinking of you, until I spring into
consciousness and you are before me as clearly as the road I
am driving or the fork I raise to my mouth—that close, that
immediate, I love you so."

And I have written to her: "Come here and I will make
you lamb with anchovy butter. Courgettes and tomates
provençal. Soupe de poissons. I will wrap you in French cot-
tons. I will bathe you in perfumes made from flowers not far
from here."

I have come to Vence, a small resort town, ten kilometers
from the sea, between Nice and Antibes, and I am sitting at
the bar called La Régence.

La Régence. Everyone here is sitting under white umbrellas, drinking their drinks, tossing their heads, talking about
le cinéma or la poésie, or the great thinkers of France, in this
beautiful place ten kilometers from the sea.

It had been a moody June, a month of cold and rain and
wind, but now the luck has changed and everyone is out in
full force to celebrate, to talk, talk, talk, to flirt, to languish in

heat and light and I am caught in it all, in a whirl of polka dots and lace, in high heels and perfectly shaped legs, of light and stripes and sunglasses. Ooh là là! At every table, salut! Ça va!

Waiters and waitresses glide by with trays of many-colored drinks. The drink that is grenadine and beer, an intense rouge, the bright green drinks of menthe and the yellow citron pressé. The cloudy drink that is pastis. And vin rosé. Les glaces fly by. Marvelous ice cream concoctions arrive at the marbled tables, topped with fan-shaped cookies like wings.

Vacationers pose for photos: the small adored dogs on every arm. "Tootsie, viens!"

Children run around a circular stone fountain. Old men race by on mobilettes. People pass carrying gâteaux and extravagant bunches of flowers. And on the street the large, expensive cars of summer drive by slowly for all to admire.

The young are engaged at every table in animated intellectual conversation. "Mais oui! Mais non! Mais bien sûr! Voilà!" They fling around cigarettes and run their hands through their tinted hair. During a lull they look around. They are not afraid to stare. I feel their eyes on my exposed back, on my shoulder, my leg. My foreign face.

"Ça va?" they say. "Ça va bien," and "à demain." I love the way their voices rise at the end of their sentences, the way they sing their language.

She has written to me: "I was so sad there was no letter from you today. I wait every day for the letters to unfold, the French stamps, the pink paper. If only I could open one of your letters, put my lips against it and taste you. I must tell you, my dove, that I feel somewhat lost without you."

Pink drinks, sea green drinks float by. Children in designer French clothes dart in and out of the palms. "François, viens!" A gloriously sculpted head goes by. All kinds of hats. It's the kind of light that makes you feel like you're seeing things for the first time. And on the radio Sade sings about Paradise.

"One feels safe from grief here," I write in my notebook.

The albino midget passes and waves.

I am known as the American woman in the Chinese hat who writes.

A girl passes who reminds me of her ten years ago. She must have Basque blood, I think.

I close my eyes and picture her here, sitting under a white umbrella at La Régence.

In three months she will leave her job in finance and come here to live. We will stay in a stone house with a red tile roof. We will live on olive oil and tomatoes, bread and figs, a few small fish. We will drink rosé from Bandol, white wine from Cassis, Côtes du Rhône. I will work on my stories. Find the arrangement of words for all this. She will learn French. Learn to love this place as I have come to love it.

And I have written to her: "The dollar today is worth six francs and suddenly, mysteriously, magically, I am richer. I'm sure you could explain all this to me—but here alone, going to the bank, it feels like another small miracle in a place of miracles."

We will live safely together in a house of stone. Surrounded by a grove of orange and lemon trees. Surrounded by roses. I will live in a house in France with her. It is finally what I have come to want. After all this time.

La Régence. The plane trees cast an incredible shade. The young move in and out of light, singing American songs—Michael Jackson, Taylor Dane—this glorious day. I order another drink.

And I write to her, "I wish I could send you a hazelnut torte or a tarte citron. I wish I could send you the way the sunlight falls on the baskets of women in town, or make a gift of the sound of bells on dimanche."

I tremble when I hear a bit of Spanish, the language she still speaks in her sleep. Or when I see a cat that reminds me of our cat. To touch a cat. She will bring the cat, of course. And the absentee ballots.

And she writes: "Today Dave caught a sixteen-inch trout, that's almost twice the length of this paper, twice my poor trout that we ate on the porch dreaming of Nice. Dreaming of Antibes."

I miss her. I am acutely lonely here without her. I am the American woman, toute seule, in the Chinese hat. But it will not be long now. It's our last separation. It seems inconceivable to be apart anymore. I see it with the clarity only this kind of light makes possible. The two of us together, forever. I have given up too much, I think, to write the handful of stories I have written. I have given up too much to be the person capable of writing them. I have almost lost her as a result.

I write to her: "You are my dove. My colombe d'or."

And she writes to me: "I am going to plant the small plants we bought." She is going to make an herb garden. She is going to grow her hair.

I am trying to improve my French before she comes. Venir is to come. Choisir is to choose. Attendre is to wait.

They call the cats mignon here—little and sweet and dear, all in one word.

"Tiens!"

And she writes to me: "Be careful when the mistral comes. You know how distracted you can get. You know how sometimes you slam into every tree. Be careful. Remember how easily you bruise."

They call the children les petits. Everywhere there are French babies. Little François has wandered away from his family again, this time to pet a white bird. *"François, viens!"*

I order another drink. I stare back at the young French man when he stares at me, and I hold my notebook for courage because so much courage is required. How the day dissolves in salut and ça va. How the day dissolves in pastis. My eyes rest on a girl who has seated herself next to the young man who stares. She laughs with the carefree joie de vivre of a pretty young girl in early summer. She calls out to a friend passing through the square, "Pascal, attends!"

Attendre is to wait.

Another man comes up to me. I steer clear of desire. It's a

choice I'm learning can be made. His eyes graze my leg. I want only her now. Still I write in my notebook, "One does whatever one must. One walks through fire if necessary, through light. Attracted to it like moths. One swims in treacherous waters like poor trout, brochette. Attracted to it like salmon to their deaths."

What is this love of the illicit, the forbidden? This love of oblivion?

I'm drifting off. These strange hours of writing in the cafés and bars of Vence.

"Tu es toute seule?" he asks.

"Oui."

I feel my ankle and then slowly the rest of my body begin to go. I look back. I guess I'm curious just how persuasive this blond offering Gauloise might be.

There is so much longing in me.

"Non. Merci." I am waiting for her.

A fish, a woman, a vulture appears before my eyes. I can't stop from seeing this. A spear. Goats gambol around a dancing nymph. Fishermen devour their catch of sea urchins in darkness. I think of the great Picasso, who has given me this, painting in Antibes. It is 1946 and he has just met the beautiful Marie-Thérèse in the Galeries Lafayette and they are lying on the beach at Juan-les-Pins and they are about to go for a swim.

Something here is slightly dangerous. These strange hours of writing. Sometimes there's vertigo. Sometimes I lose the way home.

You bruise too easily. You go under.

Home. Everything had left its mark: the paper tearing, the cry of concrete, the red sign lighting the dark city that said PSYCHIC. I was too afraid there. My older brother in a white bed.

What is it that is so dangerous under this bright surface of saluts and kisses and ice cream and many-colored drinks in the dazzling afternoon?

I look up. Love should be like this: a blond boy in a striped shirt tipped back in his chair on the dazzling surface of the afternoon. A boy framed by bamboos and palms and large cars, eating a sandwich jambon. Only his eyes on my leg. Love should be like this. But it is not. Love is too imperfect, too hard. I think of our ten years together. I'm losing my concentration. I close my notebook. On the cover of a magazine at the next table it says, "SIDA: les chats aussi." One must take care in a foreign country. Without language there is no preparation, without familiarity things pop into your vision seemingly out of nowhere. Without warning, magazines like this one. "AIDS," it says, "cats too." One must take great care.

I was too afraid there. My older brother and I in a white room erasing our names page after page.

I am the American woman in the Chinese hat who writes.

Everyone here is talking. Everyone here is flirting. From this perch I can watch all the Vence regulars come and go. Names I would hope to someday know.

Vouloir is to want.

Attendre is to wait.

Manquer is to miss.

How beautiful she would look in white under a white umbrella at La Régence.

I might make her a hat from a paper napkin.

We might order an ice cream with wings.

We might practice our French.

We might tear off the ends of a baguette.

We might drink Veuve Cliquot in our black dresses and try to guess the nationalities of all the people around us.

We might even allow the mistral to make us crazy; safe with each other.

Everyone here is kissing everyone else. My waitress is at the next table taking an order. She is wearing her Day-Glo clothes, her butterfly belt, her necklace of plastic leaves and fish and spears. The bus pulls up from Nice. A man steps off, comes up from behind, and caresses her. She turns. She is wearing her favorite striped midriff top and she is in love.

Two women just off the bus from Nice sit at the table next to me. One is dark, one quite blonde. They laugh, twirl lavender between their fingers. They order two sparkling drinks and toss their heads back in the sun. They are American. It is easy to see. Here on vacation—like everyone.

They talk excitedly. I strain to hear: a concert at the cathedral, the Musée Picasso, the marché in Antibes, soaps from Marseille. They practice their French. They talk with their waitress. One feels safe from grief.

A cat, one of the hundred cats of Vence, comes up to me and rubs against my leg. It is soft, the softest thing perhaps I have ever touched. I tremble.

When I look up I see that one of the women has begun to cry. She is frightened suddenly. It's a vague feeling. Impossible to pinpoint. Her friend tries to comfort her. "Don't cry," she says. "There is no reason to be afraid. Look, we have made it!"

Everyone here is talking and flirting, kissing each other. Everyone here is laughing.

"Auto école," the dark woman says, as the driving-school car passes. "We will send you there." She reassures her as she has so many times before. She directs her gaze to a beautiful bouquet of flowers. "There is no reason to be afraid."

"Yes, of course, how silly of me," she says and smiles.

Every rose trembles.

Whatever it is has passed. I am glad.

"François, viens!" Maybe they will have a subsidized French baby. Here you are given money to make French children. They laugh.

They are not here on vacation after all. They have come to stay.

The one who was afraid tells a story. She says: "In June I went to a village a little ways up from here called Saint-Jeannet. It was raining. I stepped into the church and said a prayer. When I came out the whole town was washed in light. I watched a golden dog in the square. I heard bells as the afternoon slowly turned to evening. From a window I watched three children put on a magic show. They pulled flowers from their sleeves. Eggs. 'Voilà,' they kept saying, 'Et voilà! Magique!'

"I was still crossing out the days until you then."

The dark woman smiles. "Maybe we will live there. I think I would like to stay in France forever."

I close my notebook. I count the days like magic. This is the place we think we could love. It wouldn't take much.

I watch a flower being pulled apart. She loves me; she loves me not. In bright light I watch a woman being sawed in two. Because I do not know how to look away. . . .

She loves me; she loves me not.


## 3


Dimanche and the bells arrange themselves around the pure desire to believe. Each village rings out. Vence, Saint-Jeannet, Saint Paul, Tourrettes. I look into the faces of the faithful as we enter the ancient cathedral

Inside in candlelight, I look for Mary, her blue robe, her open arms. Elle est vierge toute pure. I memorize her flaring back, her steady gaze. Mary, our Lady of Sorrows. I ask her for peace here. I ask her for patience and courage. I allow the mass to wash over me in French. Ciel is both the word for heaven and for sky, I think. I pick words out: Toujours. Sans doute. Sans exception. L'éternité. Such beautiful words.

Last night the bicyclettes racing around and around the square in the heat. Colors. Names: Chambord, Bilot et Fils. Flags. The bicyclettes whirling. A microphone, trophies. Who can make sense of any of it? I miss her.

If I turn my head I can see the great vaulted entrance.

Bright light pours in. Luminous vegetables and fruit. Let it be
enough for now, I ask the Virgin.

Two children hold a white linen at the feet of the priest to
catch fallen hosts.

"Le corps du Christ."

"Amen."

"Le corps du Christ."

"Amen."

Dimanche and the bells. I pass a striped cat pressed
against a window screen. A red rose pulsing. In the market
framboises Vence, anchois, artichaut violets. I hold the large,
globed artichoke, the glowing tomatoes. I go into the
pâtisserie for brioche. People buy gâteaux. They'll walk
down the peaceful streets this afternoon. Bonne après-midi,
bonne promenade, bon appétit, they're all saying. Then suddenly all is quiet.

Déjeuner behind closed shutters. All the streets of France
empty. The sound of silverware, low voices. The civility of
midday. I'll never know what they say.

I pass two goats. A rabbit in a cage. A man blowing
through a reed flute on this odd, beautiful part of the planet
called France.

I wish I had someone to bring gâteau to—or a tarte citron.

Dimanche—our day to talk on the phone. You are my
dove, I will tell her. My colombe d'or. You are my framboise
Vence. How the day revolves around the hour of the call.
How the day dissolves in white wine and cassis.

Three o'clock. It is three in the afternoon here, but it is
only nine in the morning there and she's probably just wak-
ing up. She's probably just stepped from her bath. She's
wearing my white bathrobe. She's opening the Sunday paper.
She's petting our cat. She's drinking too much coffee.

I love her.

When I dial the number I am already drunk. A thousand
centimes, those little beautiful coins I still haven't learned to
spend, fall from my pockets. They shine like gold.

The miracle of her voice inside this glass booth. It's a

shock every time. The miracle of her voice as I look out at the olive trees, the fig trees. The figs just beginning. I tell her all about my week. I can't stop talking. English! I tell her about the Arab music that sometimes snakes around the corner of the old town. I tell her about French pizza, soap from Marseille, about the bicyclettes. She is silent. Talk to me, I say. "Qu'est-ce que c'est?" I ask. "What is it? Last night the bicyclettes—"

"I'm seeing someone else," she whispers.

"No, I don't believe you."

"It's true."

And then she begins. She says she can't stand the separations anymore. She says she can't believe she's put up with so much. She says something about all my affairs. She can't go on. She says she loves me but she is worn out. She can no longer be a slave to my genius.

"My *genius*? What genius?"

"I need a break for a while, that's all. I thought you'd understand. After all we've been through."

"I don't understand."

She says something about my usual anger and arrogance "on display."

I can't match this voice with anyone. I can't reconcile the things she is saying with the brilliant day. Through the glass I watch women with flowers. Gloves. All I can say is I don't believe it. "I don't believe you."

She says I never loved her enough. She says I've been very cruel. She begins to list my crimes. But I scarcely remember being that woman.

I hear the limits of love in her voice. A pact being broken.

And then she is gone. Somewhere far off there are more bells. Centimes fly around my head like some incomprehensible future. I close my eyes and see colors. Last night the bicyclettes—

Look at them: They have lived a sort of café life. Wandering from one sorrow to the next—the white room, the blind eye, the red sign. Wandering from one song to another. From bar to bar. Sitting under umbrellas. Drinking drinks. Glasses of grappa. She is writing everywhere on scraps of paper.

They draw a picture of a stone house on a napkin. "Maybe there could be a real home here!" they say. Maybe they could be happy. "Don't forget the fireplace. And the attic room—just large enough to write." Outside she draws cats. An olive tree. A fig tree. She labels the cats, Coco, Mignon. She holds it up and they admire it. They will carry the picture with them as they walk the streets of the small villages.

They wouldn't need much, would they? A few small fish, an arrangement of figs. A little paper. A handful of words.

The stories said: I exist. Even though they were mostly sad. It was something. The stories said: I am alive. They were a way to survive.

Someone puts on *Madame Butterfly* in the square and they cry.

Toujours. L'éternité. Sans doute.

"I love you," she says. She's afraid that it's already too late—the one who is afraid.

She feels the afternoon in their embrace. The stone walls. The black fruit. The figs already falling. She writes: déjà.

"Don't be crazy," the dark woman whispers.

What is it they can't seem to get right?

They laugh. Even though it's been difficult—she's been difficult, they still want to be together starting over again in an open square, en plein air.

They study their house. She draws them in the attic window. Maybe they are going to be OK. "Don't cry," the dark woman whispers. "Look, we have made it!"

There's very little to say about the days that immediately follow. They are filled with what one might expect—anger, sadness, paralysis.

Melancholy music on the French radio. Stupid songs that are capable of making me cry. Every song seems to be for me, even the ones I can't translate. I understand minor chords; they are the same in every language, the longing voice, the voice lingering on the single half note, where I live suspended.

Is that rain? No, it is the water boiling.

Is that the magpies? No. My God, that is me.

I left often, sometimes for months, to write. I seduced her brother. I slept with the next-door neighbor. I slept with everyone. Often I was cruel, it is true. I was too moody—too angry, too afraid. I was never satisfied. I never loved her the way she needed to be loved.

I am tired. I will live to be old, I think. I will live to pay for every crime. Even the minor ones. Among the minor ones: I never learned to drive. I never could do the bankbook right. I wouldn't talk about the movies after the lights came up again. I couldn't talk about them, I don't know why.

In my notebook I write: "She was afraid of the woman and her many moods. Her unpredictability. Her often volatile and violent nature. All her silences and retreats. The first woman mistook this quality in the second woman for genius." I laugh out loud. The romance of genius—because what other explanation could there be?

You bruise too easily, I think. A long history of manic depression. A long history of sadness. Everyone here is laughing.

What is this pervasive feeling of danger? Of doom? A woman, a bed, a half-eaten loaf of brioche, many empty wine bottles, a swirl of vomit, the radio playing its handful of sad songs, a notebook.

The word *genius* catches fire in her head. *What genius?*

And I'm seeing things now: A man in a room reads the endless rows of deaths with his magnifying glass. Consoling to him in an odd way. The son kneels before the ruined fruit of his desire. Waves from a remote country. It's so far. She sews me a costume of sequins and black feathers. And Lola in a black dress.

I sleep badly when I sleep at all, wake myself from every dream—is that you, Lola? Is that you, older brother? He rotates the glass globe of his eye. No. It is only the magpies tearing apart the dawn.

# 6

After many days, I don't know how many, I decide to get on a bus and go somewhere. Get up now, I think to myself, or not at all. You go under. You never come up. I open my notebook: "One wants to be in love through this with anything," I write, "and she chooses Nice, or it chooses her, that deliriously beautiful city by the sea. If anything is certain it is this: every time Nice will take her breath away. She stares out at the incredible color of the Méditeranée. She hears the sound of water over stones. She sits there hour after hour. She counts the palms on the magnificent promenade. She wonders if there is a logic of beauty. She counts all the blue chairs.

"From the guidebook she reads, 'Nice industries are olive oil and flowers, perfume, crystallized fruit and macaroni,' and she thinks, what could be better than this? She writes them down in her notebook."

Italians pass. They say Nizza, as if in a dream.

I hear the sea rushing over stones.

I walk into the old city. I walk into the countless churches. I write: "I step from light to darkness to light. All the angels watch me. All the angels of Europe, tell me, if you know, yield some clue as to why this cannot be." Angels of France, comfort me.

I propel her forward. Move now, I tell her, or not at all. Look over there. I feel the flow of my desire. Là—up the stairs.

"She follows a young woman in a blinding white dress into the new city. Into American Express. She overhears her changing money, picking up a ticket. An American. She follows her into an English-language bookstore. Watches her pick up Walt Whitman, Elizabeth Bishop, Wallace Stevens. She is in love with all the right people. She follows her into the Prisunic. Watches her buy plastic dolphin combs for her hair. Next she goes into the market, asks for avocados. She explains she is from Californie and she is un petit peu homesick."

I walk up to her. I tell her I am an American. She's pleased. She has come from Cologne where she still has some family. She is just passing through. She tells me she is a writer. She writes poetry. She has studied with all the great teachers from America. I think her hair is the kind of blonde that shines in your hands.

I tell her I too am a writer. I show her my cahier. I tell her about my book, the first one. She says that sounds just like a book she knows and she says the name. It is the same book, I tell her. She can't believe it. Because we are in Nice, we have a salade niçoise together. We drink a bottle of wine. She is a little in love with the idea of me. She loves the intrigue. She talks about Nice. How it seems arranged around desire. That mild and beautiful city.

I ask her where she is staying.

"The Hôtel Rivoli," she says. "You would like it there." Because she knows my book, she thinks she knows me. And she is partially right.

"Let's see if you are right about the Hôtel Rivoli."

She laughs wildly. Suddenly she feels like she is in over her head. Her courage disappears. "Or maybe we should have another drink in the old city."

"No."

"OK." She laughs again.

We enter the Hôtel Rivoli, only a few streets away.

She quotes poetry for me. "Although I do not hope to turn again. Although I do not hope. Although I do not hope to turn."

"T. S. Eliot," I say. I love my language. I feel home in my throat, in the fluent afternoon.

She says next:

> "Complacencies of the peignoir, and late
> Coffee and oranges in a sunny chair,
> And the green freedom of a cockatoo . . .
> . . . She dreams a little, and she feels the dark
> Encroachment of that old catastrophe,
> As a calm darkens among water-lights."

We order champagne. I think of all the blue chairs in Nice. She whispers:

> "I want you to examine this solid block
> of darkness,
> In which you are imprisoned. But you say, No,
> You are tired. You turn over and sleep.
> And I sleep, but in my sleep I hear
> Horses carrying you away."

I cry. We drink.

"I thought you would be the type to cry. Your first book was so sad."

"The second too," I say. "It will be out soon."

I take the dolphins from her hair. For a moment this young Californian feels she is in the first book. The one I love would call this one of my many abuses of power.

I miss her.

"I've never been with a woman before," the poet says.

"I know," I say. "I've been watching you all day. But I think you'd like to be."

"Yes. I guess."

"With me."

"Yes."

I kiss her shoulder, part her lovely legs, sail across the perfect surface of skin, sweetly.

"Please," I whisper.

And she says: "Complacencies of the peignoir, and late coffee and oranges in a sunny chair." We make love to each lovely line.

"My God," she says. "My God," she says later that night. "No wonder men are crazy for women!" She is the type that talks. "Women are so tender, and soft and warm and wet and incredible!" She is used to describing everything. And I am on my knees this time, and she is already screaming.

In the morning an old woman brings deux cafés crèmes, deux croissants.

She comes in quickly, slows up and smiles. She has seen stranger things than two naked women in a small bed together. The room smells familiar to me. There's a warm breeze.

"I want you."

Each word a boat.

"I want you to examine." And we begin again the elaborate seduction of sadness and language.

"I want you to examine this solid block of darkness in which you are imprisoned. But you say, no."

We walk into beautiful Nice. The city opens like she did. "Nice is golden. Nice is pale green and pink. Nice is the most incredible sea blue." I am delighted to be speaking my language. "It is the person you love. It is the day off. It is macaroni. It is socca. Nice is pressed glass and polka dots. The fins of fish. The Galeries Lafayette."

Nice is golden. She is golden.

"It is sex with women," she says. It is vin rosé. And champagne. City of splendor. City of gold.

"And poetry."

We go to the beach. The French boys on the promenade

wear T-shirts that say SURF, SURF, and ROWING TEAM, and NO PROBLEM. We laugh. She quotes Rimbaud for me. She tells me the French she knows.

We do her last-minute shopping in the Galeries Lafayette. We buy lipsticks and lingerie. She's leaving this evening.

On the beach she quotes me one more thing:

> "The palm at the end of the mind
> Beyond the last thought, rises
> In the bronze decor,
>
> A gold-featherd bird
> Sings in the palm, without human meaning,
> Without human feeling, a foreign song."

She kisses away my tears, salty as the sea. "Good-bye, young poet," I say as she gets onto the plane.

Across the blue envelope of sky I write, "Be safe, small angel, take care, write well."

She's got dolphins in her hair.


# 7

The next day in Vence I go to the municipal pool. La piscine municipale.

She hears the sound of water over rocks.

She watches the French swim. Notes their preference for the breaststroke. She watches a woman in a black bathing suit light a cigarette. She feels the pervasive and strange eroticism in these days. The slight breeze presses her toward men she doesn't know. Men whose language she can't speak.

She is wearing her Chinese hat. She is holding her open notebook.

Often these days she finds she refers to herself in the third person as if she were someone else. Watching from afar.

Inventing someone to be—like everyone.

I had come to France to write stories about this coast, and the French, and the war, but since the phone call I work erratically, go to the piscine, stare out at the chlorine rectangle bordered by cypress and willow and olives. I study the perfect white tiles. I watch the relatively well-behaved French children do what they do.

"Regardes!" they shout. "Regardez-moi!"

"Nage avec les jambes!" a man calls out to his son.

I observe the particular habits of the French. The young at the poolside talking. I'm beginning to recognize the specific beauty of these people.

I write in my notebook: "Often she tried to quell sexual desire with a long swim in the pool. Often she tried to curb despair there." "You bruise easily," I write, "you go under."

I think about how the water comes up and it never goes back.

I write in my notebook:

> An arc of talent.
> An arc of sadness.
> A wave.
> A chlorine blue wave.
> A black bathing suit.
> Thunder
> The perfect stroke of the swimmer.
> Desire.
> The threat of rain.
> Then rain.
> Desire perfects the perfect stroke of the swimmer.

She watches a man slowly lower himself into water. She sees the dark swan of her desire float out on the surface of the pool.

Often she tried to hold back despair, stave off depression, with another affair. To lose herself there. In dazzling silence with a stranger. Where everything disappeared, every place, every name. Until she became a blank page.

My mind drifts. We did things together. We caught a glittering blue-green fish. We had a Spanish dinner together. We saw a black and white film in German. I don't know why I write it all down. Soon we would have been together, here. We thought we might have a child. It's useless to think of.

I write: "She yearns for the kind of beauty that could break even the heart that is already broken. A beauty that might somehow save her from the silence. A beauty that might change this sad, slowly unraveling plot."

She lowers herself into water. She begins to swim. Desire perfects the perfect stroke of the swimmer. They went to a restaurant called Rincón de España. They played the same record over and over. They watched her older brother, in a white room, die. They went to see a beautiful black and white film. It was German. Bruno Ganz was an angel.

A child floats by. It's useless to think of.

8

My mother writes:
Dearest Catherine,
The Fourth of July celebration is over. We had grilled, butterflied leg of lamb, parsleyed red potatoes, broccoli, and for dessert a large flag made of cake and ice cream. Everyone seemed to enjoy it. Your sister left the baby with me last weekend. He and I fish in Zabriskie's Pond and catch imaginary fish just like you and your older brother did.

I've been spending a lot of time quietly watering the gardens. We haven't had rain in a month and the weather has been hot. Watering is verboten, but I can't bear to watch it all dry up. The lawn is brown, that's bad enough. There are hollyhocks, sentinels of white, red and pink in the garden. Everybody admires them. Also for the first time Jacob's Ladder has bloomed. It is a cluster of delicate purple flowers with

yellow centers and the leaves are fernlike. The orange butterfly weed is in full bloom as are the Gliosa daisies. They look
like small sunflowers and make me think of you in the south
of France.

We have had to sneak water in the night to your older
brother's grave.

## 9

I go to Arles by train. Van Gogh walked there one hundred
years ago and that is good enough for me. On the train I
write her letters I won't send. I sit in a cage with five German
men who look out at the sea and then to me. In my notebook
I write: "The Young Arlesian." I don't know what anything
means. I never used to look for meaning, but now I feel that
need.

I have called in advance and reserved a room in a hotel on
the Place du Docteur Pomme. I suppose I have come to try to
get well. No weeping women here, I think, putting away the
letters I have begun to her.

I'm the last one off the train. A young woman looks at me
and immediately begins to cry. "What is it?" I ask.

"You are the last person on the train," she says in French.
"He is not coming."

"Perhaps he will be on the train tomorrow," I say.

"Non." She cries and cries. "He has said that if he was not
on this train it would mean he is not coming, never coming."

This is such a sad life, I think.

We decide to go to a café together. She orders de l'eau
minérale. It turns out he was her first lover, a painter she had
been modeling for. The man is anglais and she has learned
some English from him. She says that her heart is breaking.

I tell her the heart is more fragile than fruit. It can't be
handled tenderly enough.

She smiles. "You are very kind," she says.

She was born in the Camargue. She is seventeen. One could easily understand the desire to paint her—the thick dark hair, the full breasts and hips. She hopes one day to model in Paris. It is her dream. "I will show you the town," she decides.

Caesar made Arles a Roman colony, and the whole town seems like a vast museum. It is hers and she walks through it, majestic and damaged. We go to the Cloisters, the amphitheater, the Arènes. At the Arènes she says, "They have bull-fights here. Spanish music plays. Sometimes I can smell blood." We walk along the Rhône.

At dinner we sit at the Forum, a huge open square bordered by plane trees. Small white lights are strung up everywhere. It's still hot. A French man with a guitar sings a Simon and Garfunkel song: "I do declare there were times when I was so lonesome I took some comfort there." It's an odd thing to hear.

She talks more about the man. "He is a very great painter, I think," she says. But it makes her sad to say much more.

"Tell me something else," I say.

She tells me she rode wild horses in the Camargue as a girl. "The horses are born brown," she says, "and they turn white when they are grown. They are very beautiful. Sauvage. There are great pink and orange birds there," she says. "My father grows rice. You would like it. Maybe some-day we could go."

Il fait chaud. She has already said she is most comfortable without clothes.

"I must go," I say, "to the Place du Docteur Pomme. But tomorrow."

For a long time the next morning I watch the concierge feeding birds. Her outstretched fingers scatter crumbs. Every gesture in this light feels enormous, archetypal. I walk to the woman's house. Her name is Dominique. A thousand white wings before my eyes. "Bonjour, Catherine." We drink café on a terrace in bright light. "Il fait trop chaud," she says.

She tells me last night she cried herself to sleep.

"How did it happen, with the man?"

"Un moment." She goes into the house for a minute. "I was wearing this." She shows me a bright blue silk robe. A brilliant blue like hope. "He bought it for me. All the way from China. He began to paint, but he did not like my pose. He said to try putting my hand here," and she put it between her breasts. "Move it here, he said," and she put her hand on her thigh. Then between her legs. "He asked me to make it look like I was touching myself there. He kissed me. I had never made love before. He knew this and kissed me just slightly. Barely, barely brushing my lips. Comme ça." And she shows me. "It was like that that he kissed me at first. Later he would bruise my lips, the way he would kiss me.

"We went back to the pose. My hand here."

"Did you like that?"

"I liked it most when he was watching and I was thinking of that gentle kiss, oui. Later it was different. I longed for the time when there was only that smallest of kisses."

We go for a walk. I take her to the rented room on the Place du Docteur Pomme.

"Once he had me pose with another woman. She was fair like the English are. Like you. At first I was jealous of her. He was very wise. He saw this. He told me to touch her neck gently like the kiss had been. He said it must seem natural, relaxed. We became friends, the fair woman and me. I grew to like her very much. She was thirty-three, older. She said she had been modeling for ten years. In Paris. That often afterwards she made love with them."

"Where is she now?"

"She was about to marry. She lived with a painter in Paris. One day I will go to Paris."

"Have you ever modeled?"

"No. Je suis écrivain."

"Vraiment? What do you write?"

"Stories about love, and then love taken away."

"They are sad then?"

"Yes. They are sad stories."

"I love sad stories. Stories that make me cry. I don't know why." She thought of the painter. His name was Nigel. "You know then about sadness?"

"I am thirty-three. I am the same age as the woman whose neck you touched. It is old enough to know a great deal about sadness."

"You are more beautiful than that woman. Don't be sad now."

My hair is pinned up. She dares to touch my neck. She brushes my lips with her mouth again. "I knew nothing," she whispers, "except that Nigel had me touch her neck, touch myself and then put my finger to her lips. That is all."

"Like this?"

"Oui. I did it for the painting. It was my work. But I could never forget after that. Even though I felt honte."

"What is that?"

"Ce n'est pas bon. It's hard to explain." She puts her dark finger to my lips. We hold the pose a long time.

I take each finger gently, gently into my mouth and she lets out a small sigh.

"Un petit goût," I say. She nods. She is sweet like the ripe melons of Cavaillon. "Tiens."

"Un petit goût, s'il te plait." Her robe falls open. Her dark body gives off an extraordinary light. She seems to glisten.

She touches my neck again. She applies just the slightest pressure. Her touch tells me she wants more. She wants my mouth on her breasts. I touch her round belly. She nods. She wants my mouth to descend to that triangle, its luxurious dark. And she too needs a small taste. She grows. She grows wild. She turns from a brown horse into a white one. I pull her magnificent mane, press open her thighs. Ride into light. I savor the brilliant, the blinding, the gleaming—

Every tree bears fruit here. All afternoon we eat plums, figs. "It's my birthday," she says.

I sing her the birthday song, off-key. She laughs. "You are so lovely," I say. She is eighteen.

I run my wrists under cool water in the terrible heat of the room. I shudder with desire. Happy that there is this still.

In the night she says, "Perhaps you will write a story about me. It will be a little sad this story—but mostly no."

I smile. Yes, of course. I am already writing it.

I suck the dark fruit of our oblivion. Something opens that cannot be closed. And I am swollen with it, and I am soaked in it. "You are so delicious," I say.

"Et toi!" We are floating. I cannot say what ripens in me.


## 10


Overnight the sirocco had come driving the Sahara into France, into our throats and onto the hoods of the cars of Vence. I write her name—Lola—in the sand. The umbrellas at La Régence fly off their axes. I am happy to be back in this town I have begun to memorize. Because to know the pattern in the door or the design of stones in the street or the gratings and railings in every kind of light helps, a little.

She says there is someone else, and suddenly everything is sand.

I step into the garden of the Hôtel le Provence and order a Pernod. I study the trompe l'œil. The painted columns. They almost look real. The illusion of deep space. I can still smell the woman from Arles in my hair, on my skin. I'm alone here; no one else in the garden and I like that.

"It's my birthday," she whispers in my ear. "Do this for me. Don't move much or someone will see. Shh—pretend you are modeling. Now move your hand to your breast. Now move your hand again. I'll be watching you," she says. "I'll be touching your neck."

I wonder if someone upstairs parting the curtain watches this trembling woman as she touches herself in the jardin of the Hôtel le Provence. I have fantasized too precisely. A man appears out of nowhere. He walks through arbors, under trellises. "Excusez-moi," he says, "but I have to know, what is that scent? It is so familiar to me."

"Je ne comprends pas," I say.

The wind picks up suddenly. The wind stirs up everything. There's sand in my eyes. I hear the voice of an old woman in the next villa shouting in English, "We'll all be blown to bits!"

"Ton parfum," he says. "Qu'est-ce que c'est?" He asks to sit.

I nod.

"I ask because I am in the business of perfume. And it is making me crazy—the name for that scent."

"La Jeune Arlésienne," I say.

"Impossible," he says.

I shrug. He picks a flower in this wildly flowering place. I understand only some of what he says. He works in Paris and Grasse. He has a shop in Vence. He knows the names of flowers. He keeps saying "formidable." Everything's "formidable."

"La Jeune Arlésienne." He writes it down in a small black book. "C'est français?"

"Oui, of course! I can't believe you've never heard of it! What kind of parfumeur can you be? Name les fleurs, s'il vous plaît," I say, "if you are such an expert."

He tells me he has a wife and child. A lover in Nice. A lover in Paris. He takes my wrist to smell "La Jeune Arlésienne." He puts his mouth to my wrist. "It's salty," he says. I shudder; I don't know why. It's the light I guess, it's the flowers; it's the lie. It's the sudden void Lola's made, I think, that I'm trying to fill.

"Come up to my room," he says. I feel the dangerous urgency of the afternoon.

"Fill me," she whispers, "like sand. Close the shutters," she tells him. "I want it dark. Close them now. Take off my dress. Vite."

He's amazed at the person this desire has made her. "Les

américaines," he says.

When he gets off her clothes the room fills with the scent. He knows it now.

"Hurry," she says. "Faster."

And she's amazed at his stamina, at the level of his passion, his inability to stop.

"Stop. You're hurting me," she says finally.

"Encore," he says.

"Non." She wants to leave, but instead she smokes cigarettes. She must stay, of this I am sure.

On the bureau cologne, gum, keys, perfume samples. She picks up his key chain. "What is this?" she says.

"Comment?"

"F. N. What is it? What does it stand for? F. N. on your keys?"

"Front National," he says.

"What is that?"

He whispers—as if someone may be listening. "A political party."

Suddenly it all makes sense. Le Pen's party. France for the French.

"You are a fascist then?"

"Non."

"Oui. You are."

"They say we are fascists mais ce n'est pas vrai."

"Si, c'est vrai."

She tells him she is going to see Michael Jackson in Nice. He says he hates "les noirs."

Sand covers the bed. Sand covers the streets of France. The Sahara he can't keep out.

She tells him she lives in New York. He says he hates New York. "Beaucoup de juifs." He would like to what? What is he saying? Kill the Jews? Cut down the Jews? She tells him all her friends are Jews. She tell him she hates Le Pen.

He smiles. The very name seems to arouse him. I know what this passion in him is now. This intensity. He is so ugly suddenly. So large with hate.

"Perfume!" I laugh. I can say anything I want to him. I can insult him in every kind of English because he understands nothing. He kisses me hard. I know what he is and I allow him to do this. To fuck me over and over and it is not even to save my life or bring meat to hungry children or get a secret.

For a moment I am afraid, not of him, but of myself. I am frightened in the moment I realize that I don't care what happens to me anymore. It's what makes me move.

"Let me out of here," I say. "Let me go." I am grateful for the rage he awakens in me. He laughs. "Non. Jamais." And he begins again.

When he is finally asleep he is like someone dead. There is sand everywhere. It is a desert I must cross. I steal away in the night. Escape from the man who sells the most exquisite scents in France. I race through the dark courtyard of flowers.

The next day what is left is the imprint of his lips, a bloody red rose, a swastika on her neck. And it makes her feel sick.

## 11

Everyone's pushing everyone into the pool today.

"Eh, doucement!" the lifeguard shouts.

Two French girls in the water rest their elbows on the edge of the pool and talk, talk, talk—just like an Eric Rohmer film.

There's a preponderance of polka dots and stripes.

A large sign in English reads: "User of the swimming pool is kindly requested to go through the dressing room and to wear the rubber bracelet permanently."

She is a long way from home.

She is sore, bruised everywhere. The man next to her stares. What does she write in that notebook, he wonders.

"Where did you buy your chapeau?" someone asks her.

"A long way from here."

"Oui?"

"In New York. In a place called Chinatown."

Over French radio she hears Jesse Jackson delivering his address to the Democratic convention. It strikes her that he could come from nowhere but her country. "Keep hope alive. Keep hope alive. Keep hope alive," he says. It makes her cry. She is homesick. She wants to go home to her.

In her notebook she writes: "One morning her American friends call." I imagine American friends. It is necessary to believe in them. I am reliant on their existence.

In the *Tribune* it says that the MacArthur Fellows have been named.

Jenny Holzer is picked to represent the USA at the Venice Bienalle. I think of my Jenny Holzer cap at home on the top shelf in my bedroom. "Protect me from what I want," it says.

"It's an odd time," the paper says, "for George Bush to go fishing."

My mother writes of a terrible heat wave. The polluted beaches. One fish dinner a week. How much I miss her. France seems filled with mothers to me, with daughters.

So many blue chairs in Nice, she thinks, closing her eyes. She says it slowly to herself several times: So—many—blue—chairs—in—Nice.

She thinks of the blonde poet. In a blur of desire she had agreed with something she did not believe. That Virginia Woolf's *The Waves* was a failure. But it's not a digression, a wrong turn; it's a triumph, something brilliant finally.

Such thoughts.

She will probably never get to tell her this.

Everybody here is speaking French. She feels the extraordinary silence. L'étranger is the word for foreigner. It is also the word for stranger.

How she suffers. And she is a little in love with it. This romance of sex and sorrow.

She brings upon herself the end, they're all saying.

Everyone's pushing everyone into the pool today, Lola.

She wants to go home. She wants to go home to her. But she is not there. So many blue chairs.


## 12


"Attendez! Mademoiselle! Attendez!" a rasping voice calls out to me. "Young lady!"

I turn.

"*Are you English?*" she calls out.

"No, American."

"Oh, an American!" She is the woman who lives in the villa next to the Hôtel le Provence. "Come in," she says. "Come in. Don't be shy, dear. It doesn't really become you."

Her name is Sylvia and she lives in the villa called Paradis. "We *inherited* the name," she is quick to add. "Imagine anyone calling a place this *hot* paradise. The French! It's Sylvia Byrd," she says, extending her hand. "I inherited *that* name too." She is at least seventy. She covers her neck with her hand as if protecting a secret.

"My name is Catherine. I live in New York."

"Yes, but you live *here*. I've seen you for months. A long time."

"I've come to write."

"How fascinating! Write what?"

There's a knock at the door. "Yes?" she calls through the door. "Yes?"

"It's me Miss Byrd, it's Allan."

"What do you want, Allan?"

"I'm stopping by to borrow the book you said I could look at."

"What book was that?"

"The Gertrude Stein."

"It's not possible right now. You see there's a young woman in here with a dreadful headache, so it's not going to be possible right now, but do come back!

"The soul *does* select its own society after all," she whispers.

"All right. I'm sorry," he calls in. "Tell her I hope she feels better."

"I most certainly will!" she says with her rasping cigarette voice. "That was Allan. He's Australian. Terribly nice. He's working on a play that takes place in Paris in the twenties. As if we need another! Until I met Allan I used to think Australia was a place under a lot, a lot of tables." She roars with laughter.

"And how do you like Vence? D. H. Lawrence came here to get a tubercular cure and was dead in two weeks. Monica and I tried to get the maire to do something about the house—at least to note the place where Lawrence had died—but Vence wanted nothing to do with Lawrence for years and years. There's a little plaque now.

"What did you say you write? Fiction! How *marvelous!* In that case you *must* meet C. D. Cunningham. A good friend of mine, a marvelous short story writer from London! I've known C. D. for ages. She is a dear, that one. In fact Monica used to say it was her sweetness that kept her from writing anything really good. Oh that Monica, she was shrewd!"

She slips easily back and forth in time like someone who refuses to give up anything. Monica's there and then she's not. There's a war and then the war is over. Then it is back on again. "Oh yes, I fought the Nazis in every way. One must use whatever one has. I happened to be born a ravishing beauty—I just used it for the greater good."

From what I can gather, early on she was a sort of international playgirl.

"Well let's put it this way," she says, "I played a *lot* of tennis!" She laughs and laughs.

"They put my own brother in a concentration camp, he wasn't *nearly* as deft as I was, but they released him after the king of Sweden intervened on his behalf. The king of Sweden and I had been mixed double partners. Indeed!" She laughs again.

I can see she was once that great beauty. She has the audacity of someone who was once beautiful and continues to see herself that way.

"Fiction!" she says. "How terribly exciting! One book already and you can't be more than twenty-five," she says. "I love that about you Americans. You *think* you can do *anything*!

"Oh, Monica would have liked you. She was a book reviewer for the *London Times* for years! How do you like my house? I'm afraid that it's rather packed with the work of all our local artists. You see I love artists. Vence, Tourrettes, Saint-Paul—these towns are about as perfect as you can get, but the art is quite another thing." She grumbles to herself. "Well *someone* has got to buy their work," she says. "People aren't exactly queuing up for it. I met many young painters and sculptors in Tourrettes. I had a flat there when I first came to France. Gone are the days of Signac, Modigliani, Bonnard. Gone are the days!

"How is your French? Do you plan to stay? You don't know! I'm going to have to read your tarot cards one of these days. Then we'll see what's what."

As I'm getting up she whispers, "I've always wanted to write poetry. You know I was a friend of Eliot's. Next time you come I will tell you about Eliot!"

13

In my notebook I write:
You do not know that I have been to Nice.

I do not know if she is beautiful.

You do not know that today I broke out in hives after swimming in the sea.

You are not here to put a cool cloth on my face and speak

softly to me and watch the hives fade.

I do not know if you are worried about your job. I do not know what your boss says to you or what you say back.

You do not know when my period comes. You do not know that I get it now every two weeks.

I do not know how long your hair has grown.

I do not know if you ever planted the basil and oregano and thyme we began in the little sod pots.

I do not know what your nights are like.

I drink pastis. I eat pâté now.

I do not know what she whispers to you or what you write in your journal.

It's a year of thirteen moons. Two full moons last month.

You do not know that my watch fell on the tile floor and broke. The big hand has detached itself from the little hand.

I have seen the albino midget.

I try to avoid the melancholy French radio. I resist seeing my heart as the crushed pigeon in the street, in the small birds spinning on their spits.

We did things together. We had fun.

My mother has written me that many of the beaches on the East Coast are polluted. Waste washes up on every shore.

You do not know that I have sat in the Square Jean Cocteau in Menton.

There are lemon trees there.

You do not know that I have been to Arles.

You do not know that I've lost my sunglasses again and have opted to live in the light.

I do not know if she is beautiful.

I still dream of you every night.

Early one morning her American friends call. They have
settled into their perfectly restored perched village only minutes from Vence. They ask questions and she answers yes.
Yes, you must go to the Colombe d'Or. Yes, you will watch
the men play boules. You will love the views. Yes, if you are
lucky you will see Yves Montand. There is a Léger show at
the Fondation Maeght, she tells them. Yes.

Her American friends, two lawyers from New York, insist
on seeing her. She goes to visit. "It's over," she says. "That's
all. I'm not a lot of fun," she tells them.

They talk about the weather endlessly, though there is
nothing really to say. She's gotten tired of day after perfect
day. But there is no way to complain.

I know why they are here. They have come to help her. To
stave off something. They mean well.

It is over, she has told them. That is all. They walk down
the rue Grande carrying their Michelin guide. They walk into
the church and read from the book: "There is near the font a
fifteenth-century alabaster Virgin, and at the far end of the
aisle a painting attributed to Tintoretto of Saint Catherine in
a red cloak, sword in hand."

She cries. She doesn't know what to believe anymore. She
writes: "You do not know that I have been to Saint Paul de
Vence. The choir stalls are seventeenth-century carved wal-
nut."

They've got to agree, she's difficult these days. Back in the
house they've rented, American music plays.

She cries.

They don't know what to do for her. They are here on vacation, after all.

They've brought her the books she asked for from the
apartment in New York. She knows they saw Lola when they
were there. She sees it in their faces. She doesn't ask anything.

They go to watch the men play boules. She orders a pastis.

There is so much darkness in her, even today, on a terrace in bright sun.

She thanks them for the books and returns to Vence. It is not far.

"This is the house they almost lived in," she writes. "There the striped cat. The pulsing rose.

"This is the stone house they wanted to believe in. The field of herbs. These are the streets they almost loved, the way they almost chose to walk.

"This is the vine they almost staked their life on. The tomate, the courgette, the aubergine.

"Here, a few figs in a dish. They thought it might be enough once.

"This is the dusk they thought they could love."


## 15


Her ghost meets me when I open the book from home. It is her copy of *Death in Venice*, the one she read in high school, in the years before I knew her. It is stained with suntan oil. She must have read it on a beach somewhere and imagined that water city.

I leaf through it. She writes "important" in the margin next to Aschenbach's musings on the artist. "Who shall unriddle the puzzle of the artist's nature? Who understands that mingling of discipline and license in which it is so deeply rooted?"

She scrawls "important" again on page twelve. She puts a question mark next to the word *puerile*, which she has circled. It is coupled with sensuality, underlined.

Puerile means childishly silly, Lola. It means juvenile.

Also there's a question mark next to "very much he feared being ridiculous." For what to this dreaming teenager could seem ridiculous in Aschenbach's delirious quest for beauty in a dying city?

"Solitude gives birth to the original in us," I read, "to beauty unfamiliar and perilous—to poetry. But also it gives birth to the opposite: to the perverse, the illicit, the absurd."

I am toute seule. And I am afraid.

"The trip will be short and he wished it might last forever."

I picture her as a girl on a beach reading *Death in Venice* and taking notes, underlining, making comments in the margin. And one day I will love her.

## 16

I swim every day at the piscine municipale. I realize, more than anything I am coming to resemble a resident of Vence. Except for the cahier I carry, I am just like everyone else. My red rubber bracelet. My towel and chapeau. My tolerance of the heat.

My first French comes back: plié, jeté, arabesque. A child in ballet class.

Little girls walk by demurely in green and pink suits. The backs are scooped and there are little bows. Some of the suits are yellow, with blue polka dots. And the boys in their checks.

The children step over me. They love to come up close. All kinds of children, I notice, are drawn to me. They cling so tenaciously. I think of the fierceness of children. Their tiny hands. Their songs.

You are like a child, she always said. You are acting like a child.

A little girl is waiting for her mother who is coming at cinq heures et demi. In the meantime she's adopted me. Her bathing suit says SMILE in English. Summer of smiles. She skates along the smooth tiles.

A teenage girl holding a book, Zola I think, passes. She still has braces. She has a beautiful body.

Next to me, the British. Why is Vence so filled with British? The British—reading their Sidney Sheldons, demanding that everyone speak their peculiar English. Their white pants and loafers, their cigars. I don't like them one bit.

I take out my French workbook. It is called *En France avec Nicholas*.

I think of the word *avec*.

I am just trying to feel at home here.

Nicholas is at the bookstore. He is trying to find les oeuvres complètes de Victor Hugo.

Nicholas is going fishing. Nicholas va à la peche. Un poisson passe. He says to his friend, "Oui, il est très gros, c'est vrai. . . . Oh regarde tous les poissons! Vite!"

Nicholas is in love. He has a bouquet of flowers for Jacqueline. Nicholas montre le bouquet. Jacqueline n'arrive pas. "Attends un peu," I write on the empty line given for my response. "Elle va venir."

"Tiens!"

Tenir is to hold.

Children race by. "Regardes. Regardez-moi!"

I notice certain words dear to the French entering my vocabulary. I "adore" the swimming pool. I "adore" la Côte d'Azur. I "detest" George Bush. Something is "bizarre" or "superb." Everything is "grave" or "not grave."

"J'arrive!" the children cry.

We thought we might have a child together.

Tenir is to hold.

Nicholas is lost. Nicholas is perdu.

Except for the cahier, and the French workbook, and the Chinese hat, and all the crying, I am just like a resident of Vence these days.

Nicholas remembers: "Quand j'étais enfant, à Pâques ma mère cachait des œufs de chocolat dans le jardin."

Translate.

"When I was a child, at Easter my mother would hide chocolate eggs in the garden."

There's a light on at Sylvia's and I decide to stop.

"*You!*" she says. "I was just thinking of you. Sit down. You're just in time for *Apostrophes*. It's only just begun," she says.

The most popular show on French television is four or five people sitting around talking about books. The most popular show in France is talking heads. A bunch of writers talking about their books led by one highly animated host, Bernard Pivot, his glasses halfway down his nose, his glasses off, waving in the air, as he questions his writers, demands, laughs, attacks—the audience enraptured. Fifty feet of books behind him. "Philosophie, poésie," the ancient and modern world. My head spins with the French. I'm not really following it.

"Are you convinced you've come to the right country yet?" Sylvia laughs. We watch them passionately discuss historical objects taking the place of religious objects. The room is action-packed. Camera one cuts to camera two. They are talking as if their lives depended on it.

"Sans doute!" Pivot exclaims, throwing his arms in the air.

Claude Lévi-Strauss is a guest. Bernard Henri-Lévy. "B. H. L.," Sylvia informs me. A novelist, Le Clézio, with his book *Le Rêve mexicain* discusses innocence and destiny. Breton is mentioned, the beloved surrealists.

"That B. H. L. knows he's good-looking," Sylvia mutters.

And there's an American, Tom Wolfe, talking about New York. He doesn't have a word of French, which they all scoff at, and he uses a translator. He talks about his book, *The Bonfire of the Vanities*. About New York—Wall Street, the Bronx.

"What do you *think* about what he's saying?" Sylvia asks, a mini-Pivot. But New York is a place I can barely call up in my mind anymore.

I speak to Sylvia in French. I envy the freedom they all speak with on the television. Me with my two or three sentence constructions, my two tenses.

They talk, talk, talk. Now about the Goncourt Prize. Passions run high. They talk about history. "Yes," Sylvia sighs, "history, always from a man's point of view. It's a lie," she says, "it's a terrible lie."

They are finally quiet. "That Tom Wolfe *looks so stupid.*" She laughs.

We talk more about the show when it's over. "You know," she says, "you speak French quite well, well not badly, but you don't understand a *word.*"

She loves writers. "Yes, Lawrence thought he was coming to get better, but really he was coming to die. There was some business of coffin-snatching—to get the body back to Cornwall."

She wants to write. "One's hidden dreams are not so hidden I'm afraid," she says. "I was very fond of Eliot you know," she whispers in the flickering blue television light. "One day I'll tell you about him."

## 18

I tell my American friends flatly that I do not love the person she most wants to be, the person she aspires to being. An ordinary person. Someone ordinary.

"It's that simple?"

"Of course not." But how to say? I think of the words in my language that have been invented to approximate this state of disorder. "Irreconcilable differences, it's called." I think of other terms invented for the unsayable: "catastrophic illness" is a way to say AIDS now, Klaus Barbie is on trial now for "crimes against humanity." All these phrases seem oddly right, today.

"No one *likes* such difficulty," the American friends say. "Maybe she needed a break."

"Of course." They don't know the half of it.

"Maybe she's had enough."

I nod.

"Why don't you just give her a little leeway? Maybe this is something she just really needs to do. Think about it for a minute, Catherine."

I look up. Shake my head. "Sorry," I say. I am making a deliberate choice. Calmly even. Though my American friends say no and stop, you do not know what you are saying.

"It's over," I say. "There is no way back there now."

While the words were never perfect, they were something. She said: love. She said: forever.

"It's over."

"No. You are wrong. It is only a fling. It's nothing."

Everything my American friends say sounds like a translation.

She follows them through the streets, weeping. They go to Les Colettes, in Haut-de-Cagnes. They read from the guidebook, "With his first symptoms of arthritis Renoir moved here in 1903, to a grove of thousand-year-old olive trees. He had three studios and was surrounded by his wife, his models, his three children and a small circle of friends, including Rodin and Maillol. Renoir lived and painted here every day for the last twelve years of his life. A painting shows the old, stooped artist sitting at his easel and working with his brush tied to his crippled hand." She cries.

They drive in the car. She walks in and out of the great churches of France. She walks from dark to light to dark again. Small white votive candles and the Virgin everywhere. The high vaulted ceilings make her feel small. It's so dark.

She remembers living in the Virgin's body. That blue serenity. She walks up and hugs her plaster robe. "Catherine," the American friends say, "No!" But she remembers being Joan, heroine of France, burning to a fine ash for the country she loved. She lights a match in the dark, remembering.

For once she'd like to understand the terrible distance in herself. She'd like to have a reason for the sadness, for the betrayal she feels.

Your older brother, they say. Something about the older brother.

The darkness frightens her when she tries to picture it. She has tried to enter France, embrace it like a lover. She has tried to love this place they don't know together, this place they will never have in common. But she can't forget. She puts both arms in the dark bath of holy water.

"Catherine! Stop!" the American friends say.

Her American friends recall the black cloak of her madness she wore everywhere. The crown of black feathers.

We'd been miserable a long time, I think. I remember the summer day we saw the bloodied bodies of cows all over the highway. A cattle truck overturned. In the sun the blood looked black. So many livers. Heads. Hooves. Hearts. We were so unhappy then. I was miserable and she was miserable and we were convinced that what we were seeing was our life together, the shape our pain took. That was years ago, in Massachusetts. "Don't look!" she cried. "But I have to look," I said.

My American friends walk with their green guides, their "we're not home here" postures, and look at me worriedly. I'm afraid of the dark, but they're a little afraid of me.

"All those white lights were people's lives," I tell them and cry. I put a ten-franc piece into the box marked "offrandes," for the souls in purgatory. "Many of those lights," I say, "are souls in transit."

We go to a small village on the coast. I think of the black madonna being carried to the sea on the shoulders of ordinary men who danced, who ate, who did not want to die. In the empty cathedral two singers rehearse French psalms at the microphone.

Sans doute. L'éternité.

On the way back we pass billboard after billboard advertising the concert Michael Jackson is about to give in Nice. On the radio I hear something about "La Maison Blanche." "Ronald Reagan." "George Bush." "One fish dinner a week," my mother writes. The greenhouse effect, many of the beaches closed. I would cry for my country, if I had any tears left. I would cry for the fear in my American friends. I would cry for my older brother. I would cry, once more, for that blood-covered road in Massachusetts.

She said: love. She said: forever. Like the songs from America said.

Back in Vence I walk to the papeterie to buy a *Herald Tribune*. All the news is sad. I'm not surprised. When I turn the page I see that Raymond Carver has died. At the end he is quoted: "We were just looking for a place where I could write and my wife and two children could be happy. It didn't seem too much to ask for. But we never found it."

## 19

Two women in the square on market day. One plays a harp, the other, bells. At their feet a sign says, "Deux femmes de 54 ans essayant de gagner leur vie dans la dignité. Bonne journée et merci à vous." At their feet a little basket for money.

The albino midget passes offering drugs. The mime troupe. The flutist standing on one leg plays a melancholy song. My older brother waves from across the remote globe.

Why is everything so sad? She held it against me, my sadness. She said she couldn't bear it anymore. You call that love?

Such sadness, such heat, such brilliant light lends an unreality to everything I see. Women rush through the square with their baskets of bread, their fruits and vegetables, before everything closes. She sits in a café in the old city and has a pastis. A huge bee buzzes around her. She begins to weep.

She has stopped believing in love. She pictures a woman, not unlike herself, not unlike herself at all, despairing in a dark room in Arles. The shutters blocking the intense

Provençal sun. She pictures a sink and a woman in the terrible heat holding her wrists under the cold water.

In my cahier I write: "She stepped into the fountain and sat there in water, one leg then the other—and the beautiful stranger looked on.

"At first she was self-conscious. At first she minded her half-wet skirt; people were gasping, she could hear them, their human sounds, but they were soon replaced by water. She went down to its dazzling center. It was not black water, as she had imagined; it was rouge. How strange. Like wine. But she was dying into it, undeniably. She noticed the feet of a woman at the bottom of the stone fountain. She saw rainbows. Pools of light. It was lovely and she felt so cool. But she couldn't breathe or lift herself. She was dying."

I am known in town as the American woman in the Chinese hat with the notebook who cries. I don't know why I write those things in my notebook.

These strange hours of writing and drowning.

I read: olive oil, flowers, perfume, macaroni, crystallized fruit.

The young wear shirts that say CALIFORNIA, SUN, SURF. Everyone here believes in California. Here it is still the place of dreams.

Les petits come out of the ballet school run by one Henriette Sondier. I too was a little ballerina once. When the next class starts I hear the first French I ever heard coming from the école de danse. Jeté, plié, pas de deux, arabesque, grand jeté, relevé. I see my round patent-leather ballet case. I touch it: it is smooth, shiny, bright. My mother is there, always waiting. I wait and watch the little ballerinas come out—as if I'll see myself again, taking my mother's hand.

"She remembers dancing the part of the black swan," I write. "A feathered cap. And wings."

The smells of the midday meal fill the square. Someone puts on Bizet.

There is so much longing in me. I feel the strange, erotic shape of each day.

These strange hours of writing and crying. The notebook says: "There is wine in that dark room in Arles. Heavy curtains to the floor—a Provençal pattern. American music drifts in."

I find myself at La Victoire, then La Régence. How the day evaporates in pastis, in red wine and a room on the Place du Docteur Pomme.

I watch from my table the same things happen every day. There is pleasure in the simple consistency of things. The things that happen over and over.

An old couple shares an elaborate dish of ice cream. Cookies like wings adorn the top.

My waitress holds up an incredible hot pink ensemble she has just bought.

The front pages of *Le Monde* and *Libération* fly by.

A gray-haired woman sits with a gray dog on her lap.

Young lovers. They look so much alike they could be brother and sister. I am beginning to recognize the particular look of these people. The French nose. The jawline. Straight brown hair.

I feel the softness of the breeze at my neck. The far-off smell of the sea.

"The woman appears in Nice," I write, "smoking a cigarette."

Blue cigarette smoke in white light. Everyone smoking at once, in a tacit agreement to die together, as if our deaths did not have to be singular, private. I believe that only I am alone.

The sound of the plane tree leaves as they fall on the marble table.

I love the beautiful surface of the impenetrable afternoon.

People fly by. I'll never know what they say.

At the next table a heated discussion on philosophie, poésie, the great novels in the French language.

A young man tilted back on his chair stares.

A certain abandon to the afternoons.

A robe of blue silk. They are in a rented room in Arles, in

the Place du Docteur Pomme, where she has come to get well. When she opens the curtains, the shutters, the sun comes back after an afternoon of lovemaking.

They walk next to the Rhône. They drink a little Côtes du Rhône as they walk. I long to look at them forever.

She's a woman I would like to love, if I believed in love anymore.

The mind touches this one afternoon, caresses it slowly. An afternoon several weeks ago, or is it longer? She's lost track. Ce n'est pas grave.

The man tilting back on his chair folds the beautiful twenty-franc notes and puts them in his pocket. He walks up to me. "Tu es toute seule?"

"Oui."

Everyone here is kissing.

"All night while the women sleep there is the sound of wheat being scythed. She dreams of a field of sunflowers, a bright yellow square hovering off the ground. The yellow makes its indelible mark behind her eyes. She feels the pressure of its touch. She remembers red dragonflies, Gypsies, miniature horses. She remembers the stories she heard about the Camargue. She remembers the room at night with the beautiful Arlésienne fast asleep."

A young woman she recognizes passes. I'm in love with her, I decide, the cashier from the Prisunic. I'm in love with the man standing here now. One wants to be in love through this. It is a small protection against the overwhelming desire to suffer.

She fingers the black plumes of her desire.

"Tu es toute seule?" he asks again.

"Oui," she says, and motions for him to sit. "Oui."

Only touch is not a lie.

## 20

All summer long I have read from the pamphlet: "Ma forêt
c'est sacrée: My forest is sacred. For a year without fire."
Here in the forest fire region. Only sun now, no water, but so
far no fires, just great heat. The air like a furnace.

Tonight les pompiers, heroes of Vence, the firemen are
having their ball. One of the biggest events of the summer.
The small white lights are adjusted. All of Vence in atten-
dance, eating merguez, drinking red wine or beer. A band
plays. I see the people who run the boulangerie, the pâtisserie, the bars. The pompiers, proud hosts, kissing everyone,
once, twice, on the cheeks. Dancing. She is in the center of the
square. He finds her easily. It takes only a minute.

He sees her, and decides he's in love. He's in love with the
woman from America. He's in love with her mane of burning
hair, her American clothes, her je ne sais quoi. After one
dance he won't let her go. He wants her. He is strong like a
pompier, she says. He wants what burns in her.

"Encore," he says. "One more. One more dance."

She is like fire. Dangerous. Hot to the touch. "Just one more."

Her American friends come to her rescue. "Ce n'est pas
possible," they say to him.

One more.

The American word *rage* creeps in, like a code between
words, a subtext.

"In America the pompiers have red trucks," she tells him.
"They are very brave. They would never hold a woman
against her will. Jamais."

He laughs.

He wants the woman who is the fire. And she, it's true, if
he can, she wants him to stop the burning. The rage. Her
American friends are afraid for her. They want to take her
back to Saint-Paul. They know the look in her eyes. But she
protests. She promises she'll be OK. She promises that tomorrow she will spend the day with them. She knows that she is
alone. There is nothing they can do to make this better.

And I admire her, this woman, for her fortitude and grace, her desire despite everything to live. Her unwillingness to give up.

She has one more dance with the man who tries to make the American laugh by saying "Coca-Cola c'est ça!" And he sings the lyrics to American songs to her, his only English. She laughs with a sort of hysteria. She cries.

"I am Joan of Arc," she tells him, "and I am on fire."

He laughs. He begs her to come with him. And she wants him now to take her to the firehouse. "The house of fire," she calls it in French. "The place where you wait for the fires," she says. "The place with the red truck."

"What red truck?"

She wants to go there with him. She wants what is still outside her control. Finally, she finds a way to make him understand.

"Oui." He laughs.

"Dépêche-toi," I whisper in the black night. Where has everyone suddenly gone? I wonder. Where are the American friends? I light a terrible match. "Dépêche-toi."

They walk in the black night with bats. She is afraid. She points to the sky.

"Oui," he says, "les chauves-souris."

She is afraid.

When they get there she looks around the large room. Where has everyone gone? "Where are the pompiers?" she asks.

"A la Bal des Pompiers, bien sûr," he says.

He holds her up against the ladder. He is strong, she tells him. But she is more strong. "Je suis plus forte," she says. "Superwoman."

"Non." He holds her tightly. He wants to keep her. Hold her down. As everyone has tried to hold her.

"Superman," he says. "Batman."

"Where is your fire costume?"

"Quoi?"

Again she feels trapped. He kisses her hard. Harder.

"Where is the pompier?" she asks. "I am on fire."

He goes into another room. He is laughing and saying bizarre things. Singing songs. That much she can tell.

"Voilà!" he says. "Le pompier est ici!" He wears boots, a yellow raincoat.

A fire burns. And I'm seeing things now: a rose, a horse, a rubber hose.

She allows him to arrange her on the bars of the ladder. On the rungs of the ladder. He opens her flaming legs. Ties her ankles and wrists with a rubber hose. He is here to save her.

She is burning. She is tied to the stake. If she could only rise from the flames.

If there was any genius at all in her she would rise from the fire like smoke. But she can't.

She's muttering. She's very strange. He doesn't care; she's beautiful. He wants to hold her here forever.

He kisses her flaming face.

Doesn't he see she's got a charred and blind eye? Doesn't he see the awful singed hair, the burning head? The red sign that says PSYCHIC?

My cahier at my feet. If I could only reach it.

"You were here to keep us safe. You were our last hope," she cries, "a pompier in a yellow coat."

Already I can predict the end. I am writing this plot—what plot there is. She is acting it out for me. Only the details are missing now.

He's wearing his black boots. His leather strap. And a hat. If she could only be spared the rest.

He needs to have her here forever.

She weeps. "Ce n'est pas possible."

She's a mouth, breasts, a few fingers. A bit of singed hair perhaps. That's all he can have. He's a blur—rubber boots. A hat. A hatchet.

If she could only rise like smoke.

"Help me," she says in English. And then, "Where is my Chinese hat?"

He laughs.

## 21

Sylvia remembers the time she saw the Doge's Palace. She remembers purple robes and jewels in the water city. Alas, she says, that life seems a long way off.

She remembers things almost no one remembers anymore. T. S. Eliot asking for prawns. She is talking in morning light against a background of astounding red geraniums.

She remembers her first love. "She had a white coat and yellow hair and I followed her. I was in second grade and she was in fifth grade. We had knitting classes. I had thick needles and white wool, but she had thin, delicate needles and pink wool and I just *adored* her!"

I think of a young girl reading *Death in Venice* and taking notes. Underlining, making comments in the margin. And one day I will love her.

She remembers Poulenc in Tourrettes writing *The Dialogues of the Carmelites* in 1955.

She remembers Dylan Thomas. "And everyone thought he could make his own decisions and knew what he was doing. No one ever told him to stop, though it was *quite clear* he was drinking himself to *death*. No one showed him the least bit of concern. We just watched him kill himself."

A gray-striped cat comes up to us. "Monica loved cats."

I tell her about the woman. I tell her about our home in New York. I tell her how we met. I tell her about our cat. I dare to touch the cat and cry. I tell her I remember making love after a night of grappa.

"I can't believe you're one of the girls!" Sylvia says. She wonders what Monica would say. "Of course I'm sorry to hear about your friend. Foolish one that one must be."

I order another Campari and soda.

"Well we just watched Dylan die. And no one said a word about it. Oh we thought we were so smart! The last time I saw him was in the street, in the rain. 'I believe I know you,' he said to me. It was just *awful*."

I guess the house we lived in in New York was also stone.

For her it had no windows or doors. But while I was away, somehow she found the way out.

She remembers Monica's hand moving to meet hers in the small guest cottage on the edge of a cliff in France. That was long ago.

The woman I am disappears in alcohol and sadness.

Sylvia's hands tremble. "What is it?" I ask her.

"I never said anything to Dylan, but I'm going to say it to you. I can't bear to see this happen again," she whispers. "Recognize," she says, "that you're in a good deal of trouble."


## 22


I picture lovers on the beach at Antibes. They are perfect in their black bathing suits, next to the blue-green water, under the hot sun. On their lips "l'amour," on their lips "Côte d'Azur." Dark glasses, Day-Glo, Picasso. They are lost in the long syllables of desire. The elongated shape of the afternoon.

I want to join them.

I enter the light that makes every one of these days more than themselves.

For a minute I forget she ever lived.

I savor this feeling, however illusory, however momentary, that life can be begun again on a beach in Antibes.

Above us the Grimaldi Castle, which has been turned into the Musée Picasso. For eleven months he worked here, filling the castle with sea urchins, with satyrs, with fishermen, with spears, filling it with his passion for Antibes, his joie de vivre.

The lovers are now on their stomachs. Goats gambol around a dancing nymph. A yellow and blue faun plays a double flute.

A small deep-sea diver passes in a striped suit, holding a plastic fork and pail for creatures. Pink, blue, and green jelly beach shoes. A poodle under a parapluie. Not a parapluie, a parasol. A tiny crab in the white netting of surf.

"A citron pressé, s'il vous plaît. Un sandwich jambon."

She could no longer live with my genius, she said. Of all the unfair things she has said, that is the most unfair. What genius?

We lived in deference around the so-called talent as if it was something that might go away or break.

I watch the lovers. From a basket they take out their déjeuner. They whisper. He sighs. Removes his sunglasses. They eat on the swollen beach. In some detail he tells her how he would like to have her.

I seduced the next-door neighbor. I made love with him all the time—when you were at work, when you were away. There's no reason to deny it.

I slept with that actor in your first film. He was very vain, you must remember. But that was when you were in film school. That was long ago.

I made love to your brother, the male version of you. He was only a child then. I left your room for his, but why? What was I looking for in the middle of the night?

I'd confess things you don't even know I did if that would help. No point now though.

Don't mistake any of it, Lola, for genius.

Think of Picasso.

Before my eyes I see the flayed head of a bull, a cat destroying a bird, a skull, a candle. A fish, a woman, a vulture appear. A spear.

The lovers, having finished their lunch, light cigarettes. I know what they'll murmur in French in the surf.

I'd like to think our hungers looked like that—enormous, incessant, but that somehow they could have been met.

I bruise easily. I go under.

"Something should have kept us buoyant—near the surface: love or salt," I write, "something should have saved us."

The lovers stagger toward water.

I want their shining bodies.

"Don't go," I say. I want them to stay. But when they come back from their swim, they pack up their things. "You two are so beautiful. Don't put on your clothes and go." But they must of course, driven as they are by pure desire. Home.

Why can't I keep them here?

Think of Picasso, that warrior, devouring, transforming everything in his path. He has just come from a long night of work and it is morning. He disappears into the sea with Marie-Thérèse, a girl of seventeen, and he is in love today with everything. Next time you want to think of genius, Lola, think of Picasso alone in his studio all night, inventing the world by lamplight.


## 23


When she gets on the phone she cries a little. "I miss you," she says.

"I miss you too," I say.

"I love you," she says.

"Say what you like."

She talks about Martin Scorsese's *Last Temptation of Christ*, just opened in New York. She asks if I remember Godard's *Hail Mary*.

"Of course," I say. Nothing is forgotten. Nothing goes away.

She thinks I should come home. She asks me how long I think I can keep running away from the real world.

"Long," I say. "Besides *this* is the real world now." I am in the center of town at the bar called La Victoire talking to her. "This is my life now."

"Your real life is with me."

"No."

"I want you to come home. Coco does too."

"No."

"Why have you pushed me so far away?" she asks. "Why have you led us here by the hand? You pretend I have left you. But it is you who has gone. Who goes now." And then it begins. She says I have taken my mirror and dolls, my photos and lipstick, my colored pens, my baby genius, my hat. I have taken them to some dazzling and final place, where I believe I will be safe. "Say something," she says. "You know I am right. You are cutting everyone out."

"That's not true."

"You are cutting off each way of escape. Please," she says, "say something."

"Good-bye, then."

I sit at the bar called La Victoire and open my mail. She has sent me the obituary of Raymond Carver from the *New York Times*. It is the only article she has sent me all summer. It reminds her, I know, of all deaths; Raymond Carver, whose work she loved when we were younger, more hopeful. Not long ago we heard him read in New York from his book *Cathedral*. Now he is dead.

As I begin to read the obituary from the *New York Times*, plane tree leaves fall.

"Why are you crying?" the albino midget, one of the Vence regulars, asks me.

"I am crying because of a phone call," I say. "And because another writer has died."

I speak simple French and simple English and am understood. It helps to contain the chaos of the phone call. The chaos I feel after reading the article in the newspaper.

"Where is your chapeau?" he asks.

"I don't know."

I am the woman who usually wears the hat. The woman who writes and who cries. I remember the night we saw *Hail Mary*. I remember the night we drank grappa. I remember many things still. And I am grateful for that.

Tears fall to the page. I write with felt-tip pens and the

pages bleed. Tears erase each sentence as I write. Tears turn the plane trees into clouds of green. Tears cloud the pastis. Tears turn the bus to Nice into a moving blur. A sort of box.

A Cavaillon melon goes by. Tears hold the round melon up in the arms of the man who also carries deux baguettes.

Tears water this place with no rain. Tears could not put out the fires I've heard come here.

The albino midget sits and watches me cry.

Why is everything so sad? Wine drips down my leg.

She remembers all the years in the small apartment in New York. Where she despaired at the limits of words, paint, musical notes. Standing at the edge of the room, in the corners of madness, while the dark woman looked on sadly, helplessly.

She couldn't live with the sadness anymore.

You call that love, Lola?

She weeps at the limits of love.

"A demain, Catherine," the albino midget says.

Who ever heard of a person called Clover?

Elle est complètement folle. I know that's what they're all saying at this point. She's losing her mind. She's losing everything she ever believed in.

And it's true, she walks the streets with a certain resignation. Braced for what will happen next. And what will happen next? Yesterday she lost her hat. Things disappear in this heat. It's over a hundred degrees every day. But still she carries her ragged notebook.

They've stopped asking if she is en vacance. No one en vacance cries or writes that much. They would prefer it if she were. What is she writing in that notebook? They would prefer it if she were anglaise ou suédoise. There's something bizarre about an American writing in a notebook and crying. Something unpredictable in her, deranged.

Elle est complètemente folle. Elle est seule. Elle est belle. I am still trying to give her a firm identity. The American woman in the Chinese hat who cries and writes. It is not possible to survive otherwise.

She is trying to free herself from chronology, from inevitability—from pain. So what if she can't find the hat?

Every man in town looks at her. She looks back. She does not know why she looks back.

An old man—"âgé," he says, "pas vieux"—wants her to spend the night with him and the next day he will drive her to the mountains to see the beautiful fleurs.

"No, merci."

Cherchez le chapeau, I write.

She sees the purple silk arm of an aged parisienne against an olive tree in Vence, the place she has come to each summer for years.

She sees children running around a circular stone fountain.

She thinks it is beautiful here. She feels safe.

She sees waiters and waitresses glide by with trays of many-colored drinks. She feels dizzy.

She sees the large, expensive cars of summer.

*Libération* flies by, *Le Monde*. A French scientist has discovered that water has a memory; it's the big news here.

She passes the papeterie. On the cover of *Nice-Matin* it says, "Michael Jackson, le concert de l'année."

Everyone here is kissing everyone on the cheeks. It's another dazzling, perfect day.

Someone walks up to her and hands her the hat. It was left last night at the Bar Clémenceau. It hadn't moved. The French don't steal hats. The French don't need to nail down the blue chairs on the Promenade des Anglais in Nice. Merci, she says. Merci beaucoup.

She remembers the times it was too hot to move out of the stone house at midday. But wasn't that only today? What's wrong with her, she wonders?

I remember New York in the rain. I remember everything. I remember the day I raged at the limits of words. The way the woman in the room cowered.

I remember a black and white film in German. Bruno Ganz was an angel.

Everything comes back, even the hat.

Even water has a memory they say.

I think of a woman's dark hair growing long without me in another country, and I am reminded of all the times I had to move away from what I loved.

She asks if I remember when the writer read his story "Cathedral," at the bookstore near the apartment.

Nothing is ever forgotten. Everything comes back.


## 24

The woman appears again in Nice at a large stadium in a black dress smoking a cigarette. Draped across the arena is a banner that says "Bienvenue Michael." Thousands are waiting for the American to appear. She smiles. She is pleased that somehow she has gotten herself here to the top of this hill in a navette, that is, a small shuttle bus. They had misunderstood her; they had thought she was asking for a turnip.

People mill around the stadium in the hours before the concert de l'année begins. The well-behaved French children have turned into well-behaved adults. They don't really drink or take drugs or shout. Imagine fifty thousand French people not eating or drinking. Imagine fifty thousand French and no chiens!

A Swedish investment banker has come, he says, so that he can tell "future posterity" about this. He tries to pick her up. He writes his name and address in Stockholm in her cahier. Don't be ludicrous, she thinks. She has not come all the way to France, to the top of this hill, to convene with a Swedish yuppie in need of solace.

She takes her cue from the cypress and becomes singular again. She is toute seule and she likes that.

She recalls yesterday's papers. A photo of Michael Jackson rushing into the Hôtel Negresco on the Promenade des Anglais with a handkerchief over his face; "I just want to breathe air," he says. We've heard he sleeps in an oxygen chamber. We've heard he's obsessed with the bones of the Elephant Man. We've heard he's more crazy than anything we could imagine for him.

Diana Ross and the Supremes over the loudspeakers singing, "Where did our love go?"

Sing, dance, Michael, show the French this night. He is an American and the woman is surprised to feel some genuine pride.

He appears. A silvery blue blur; he's no bigger than an inch, but we can watch his enormous image on four huge video screens.

She sinks into the music. She's struck by the sheer drive of his voice. It makes his oddly moderate, even slow-paced songs seem faster, more urgent. His voice on top. It pushes, it rises, the incredible instrument of his voice. And then he begins to dance. He freezes midstep. Dances again. He sings: "She was more like a beauty queen from a movie scene. . . ."

Imagine fifty thousand French singing along with their accent, "Billie Jean is not my love." Imagine fifty thousand singing "Dirty Diana," and holding their noses. They've translated "dirty" as smelly. I think of all the things I can't tell her anymore. He sings old Jackson Five songs. He's not wearing his glove, but something, maybe Band-Aids on the tips of his fingers. The French cheer. His show is neat—neater than he is, less eccentric, well-rehearsed with no real surprises, something the French hold in high esteem. Something they'll call his "professionalism" over and over. He is very professional. Still he is wonderful. He transcends his own desire for convention. I watch him move. I watch him move us all.

I am so at home, so back into something familiar by the time the three hours have passed that I've forgotten I have no place to stay. I wasn't able to get a hotel, everything complet, this big weekend on the Côte d'Azur. The American friends with the French car gone to Paris for the grande fête.

She gives me strength. A weird courage. I take the navette

back into the center of Nice. Hundreds wait outside the Negresco, that palace by the sea, where he is staying. By the time I get back into Nice Ville it is two in the morning. There are no buses back to Vence until morning. I knew that. I knew all of this in advance.

My plan is still to look for a hotel. There may have been a last minute cancellation. There may have been a man somewhere who changed his mind and decided to stay with a mistress in Germany.

Non. It is 3:00 A.M. All are complet. I think of sleeping on the beach. Sleeping at the Gare. Dancing all night. That's when I run into the three: la femme, le noir, as he calls himself, and Pascal. They're in the last hotel I go into. They're sitting near the desk like they work there. I ask if they have any rooms. You will never find a room tonight, they say in slow, perfectly legible French. "Jamais."

"Perhaps I will sleep on the beach," I say.

They get up to leave. They don't work at the hotel. They say good night and good luck and walk two blocks or so. Then they call out to me. "Mademoiselle! Come with us," they say. "You should not sleep alone on the beach."

La femme talks to me privately. "We found a room, just by chance, this morning." I'm translating. "Before that we too had to sleep on the beach. It is not that safe. Come with us. There are three beds. You can sleep with me."

I notice I say oui to things I would never say oui to in my own country. For some reason it does not seem so unreasonable. "You can sleep with us," they say. And pourquoi pas?

"What were you doing this night without a room?" they ask.

"I went to see Michael Jackson."

"We were there too."

"Do you like Michael Jackson?" I ask.

"Oui. But we work at the concerts of Michael Jackson. We sell posters. We sell tickets to people who cannot get tickets. We do a service." Their English, which they slip into now and then, is not bad.

"You scalp tickets, you mean?"

"Yes." They laugh. "In other words, we are common thieves."

They ask me if I'd like something to drink. They bring me an Orangina. It is all true what they have said. There are three beds. La femme gives me a towel, something to sleep in. They are so kind, so generous, all three of these thieves. I think to myself, I would not be that kind. She puts on a Janet Jackson nightshirt. I think to myself this is a Bertrand Blier movie I've seen before.

They are from Paris. They talk about their city. They ask endless questions about New York. We talk about crack, SIDA, getting visas, apartments, the topics of the day. I tell them young men die in the city I live in all the time. The three thieves listen wide-eyed.

We talk about Prince, the next person they'll follow around the world.

"We steal the tickets by spraying foam in the faces of the patrons. It blinds them for a minute and then—"

I ask them to spare me the details.

They say I can come on the road with them. We could all sleep together. It's a French movie I've seen before. "No. But thank you," I say.

"De rien. What do you say in English?"

"You say you're welcome."

They talk together in French. Pascal gives me a little kiss. He tells me the word for it. La femme moves to another bed and opens her Flaubert. The noir says he wants to come to New York. He wants to improve his already good American. And then suddenly the two men and I are in the same bed. Pascal puts on a condom. "OK?" he says, and I am saying oui and we are in the thick of lovemaking all of a sudden. The noir quietly holds my ankles and watches. La femme with her Flaubert looks on. The noir kisses me on the lips, but asks first if I mind, explaining that he is black. I laugh. He is putting on a condom and he is next. Afterwards I move to la femme in her Janet Jackson nightshirt. They're only children really, twenty and twenty-one, they said. "Moi?" she says. "Oui, oui!" the two shout encouragingly to her. She agrees good-naturedly, because thieves are like that I guess. And then I am with the noir encore and Pascal is laughing and laughing. "Vite! Elle est fatiguée. Jouis!" "Oui, je jouis," the noir cries. And in one moment it seems we are falling asleep. La femme first. She says "de l'eau" in her sleep. Does she want water, I ask. "No," Pascal says, petting my head. "She is dreaming."

We have breakfast in bed. La femme departs for destinations unknown. We tell her that she said de l'eau in her sleep.

We eat croissants, drink café. On a napkin they draw me a map of France. They love their country. They show me their favorite regions. They tell me how the landscape differs, the weather. They show me places I must see. "Here, they speak perfect French," one of them says. In a few months they will be back in school.

I tell them I've got to leave. I tell them thank you.

"You're welcome," they say. "And thank you too."

"De rien."

"We will see you in New York!"

And suddenly she is back on an unknown street in bright light. The huge head of Michael Jackson on a billboard presides over the old city. She smiles, believing that somewhere someone is still watching her. Telling her story. Arranging the thieves already on the bed for this strange narrative. She feels protected a little, still safe.

She picks up a *Nice-Matin*. The headline says, "48,000 fans hier à Nice." She gets on the bus back to Vence. Over La Baie des Anges small planes fly with their messages, "Carrefores, Antibes, Nice, ouvert 15 août." Tiny silver jets fly through haze. Balloonists drift down toward the azure coast.

Where did our love go? I think, looking out the window.

I close my eyes and see that the famous, troubled American man has stepped out of the beautiful pink and green palace, unseen, and strolls out onto the beach.

# Part Two

# 1

She had been sure she would live long. Now she wonders. One feels the danger in these days. But she realizes she's not afraid of anything anymore. She loves the edges of things. She loves the danger. Light holds each thing: the cat, the baguette. Every tree bears fruit here, she thinks. Every rose pulses.

It is a day that later she imagines she will recall on her deathbed. Everything trembles. Everything seems heightened, precious, archetypal. At the cemetery flowers float in their watery globes. C'est trop.

She's turning a strange corner. She is being drawn, called by light. She follows. Pulled toward the far end of the town she now acknowledges she loves. She trembles. She passes shining fish in barrels. Olives. She passes the cathedral. Mary in her blinding, blue robe. The attenuated Christ on his enormous wooden cross, still suffering in the light of this day.

She is preparing for something; it is impossible to know what. Perhaps she is already saying good-bye. She walks slowly through the agony of the dazzling afternoon. She looks at the rose trout, the crevettes. She calls up the rose light of the Matisse Chapel. She wonders whether long ago she hadn't entered some secret pact. She thinks of Aschenbach: "The trip will be short and he hoped it might last forever."

She walks toward her desire. And today she feels like her

desire will meet her. She sees a fountain, and she stops. She is
unable to move. She stares. Though she imagined herself to
be prepared, she is not. She gasps. He is drinking from the
fountain, lowering his head to the luminous stream of water.
Dipping his hand in the liquid light.

He is shocking, like the Méditerranée. The eye widens, the
heart grows to accommodate such beauty. She sits at one of
the tables that circle the fountain. She collapses and realizes
for the first time how tired she is. These strange hours of
writing and crying have taken their toll. She knows now because, for a moment, she can rest. His is a beauty so perfect,
so complete, that it makes all else seem inconsequential.
Nothing else means anything. Nothing else matters. With a
savage turn of his dazzling head the rest of the world turns
black.

She gasps. She had not expected to meet this strangeness
so soon. Nothing in this vast place of beauty approximates
the beauty of this one young man in a Kenzo T-shirt who
leans against an amber wall in the light of the Côte d'Azur. It
is a perilous, treacherous beauty. He is drinking from the
fountain. The water pours into his mouth. I wonder if I cry
out.

She thinks that she is happy and finally prepared to die.
She can't take her eyes off him as he dips one hand then the
other again into water in the beautiful forever of the perfect
afternoon.

He is beautiful like a girl, she thinks. She watches the water pouring into his mouth. He turns and moves back to the
amber wall. She clutches her notebook for courage. A god in
a cathedral of light.

The heart grows. She feels safe. She enters this fully, feeling there is nothing else to lose, though somewhere she
knows it is not true. His is the kind of beauty she thinks that
could break even the heart that is already broken. Suddenly
everything is dangerous again and she is afraid. Though it
has been the thing she had wanted, wanted *more than anything*, now that she sees him, now that she has come face to

face with the thing she has longed for most, an object of obliterating desire, she is frightened. She is afraid of such oblivion. She feels the undeniable tragedy of the dazzling afternoon.

He does not need to be made over, transformed, changed. He is whole. There is not one thing she would change. But perhaps—perhaps. She is of two minds. Turning away and then looking back—she feels fearless again. It is the sort of beauty that reminds her of the eternity in herself. Some wild and perfect hope, some singular dream that takes away death's power. One man by a fountain obliterates it all. She studies now the intense stare, the straight nose, the long dark hair. "Cheveux longs," she writes in her cahier. The part of her that still writes. She notices the lovely jawline obscured by long hair and then revealed again as he rakes it back from his face.

Describe more, the part of her that still believed in words thought. "The elegant body." Describe this grace. But nothing she could come up with could do him justice.

I had wanted, I had asked, to be broken into pieces, smashed up, rendered senseless—because there had been too many sensations. But now that it was happening I was scared. "J'ai peur," I wrote next to "Cheveux longs" in my notebook. Cars were passing. A whole way of life was passing as I sat there.

She tried to call herself up once more as a little student of ballet, walking to class next to her mother. She tried to picture herself putting on her ballet shoes, then doing a plié in first position. An arabesque. She tried to see herself making shapes in the air. Impossible, she thought, that she was ever that child.

Still looking at the image in front of her she tries to picture next that dancer grown, a woman who had committed many crimes, grave offenses. That too did not seem right. Nothing she could come up with about herself seemed quite right in his presence. Such beauty asks, demands that one look again, reassess, see a new configuration. She sighed, hoping she would feel free, released. But she did not feel free, she felt deranged. She trembled. She was accommodating the knowledge of his existence.

I needed the kind of beauty that renders all other things meaningless. That was the kind of beauty I longed for and sought. I was looking for a loveliness I had known in women and was beginning to recognize in some French men. But this—I wasn't expecting this.

"In the beautiful forever of the perfect afternoon a man stands by a fountain."

She half hoped that he would not notice her. She half hoped he would not speak.

When he turns away she realizes she would enter this without thought of the consequences. As he turned away I knew I wanted him, whatever that would mean. And as he talked to someone next to the fountain now, I wanted him to talk to me. When he looks at me, I do not look away. I do not know how to look away. I do not know how to be a different person.

I can't pull myself away from the light in him, as dazzling as each day here. "He is bathed in amber. He is beautiful. The world is a cathedral of light."

I smile, noticing the kind of inflated language I am using in my notebook to try to approach him. A language I thought I had given up for good. I had once used such words freely. I smile, remembering that person.

When he looks away, that's when she realizes how much she wants whatever it is he will mean.

When he looks at her, she realizes that she is at the center of her own beauty. She has seen it in the faces of everyone around her. She has been accused of using her beauty recklessly and it is true in this moment she would use whatever she could to have him. She abuses her powers, only her talent she guards.

He turns away. She feels the isolation, the coldness, the terrible unfairness of a world in which he turns away. She closes her eyes for a moment. Maybe it would have been better never to have seen him. But when she opens them she is struck all over again. Arrested. She wants him to speak. When he walks up to her in the unreal afternoon light she doesn't translate a word he says. She just watches, mesmerized.

"Vous parlez français?" he asks encore, trying to get her attention.

"Non. Oui. Non. Un peu."

"Vous êtes anglaise?"

"Non. Je suis américaine."

"Américaine. Where do you live?" he asks in French.

She pauses. "New York." She remembers the dark city she was so sad in. A city so huge and strange. A city she was sure she once loved.

"And you like it there?"

She doesn't know what to answer. She nods.

"C'est très violent, non?"

"Oui. Vous habitez à Vence?" she asks.

"Oui," he says. He lives near the cemetery. He tells her he works at the galerie that faces the fountain. He sits down. Every gesture he makes is informed by grace. She realizes he has no idea he is beautiful. He combs back his hair with his hand and it falls once again into his face. It is a motion he makes a thousand times a day. He is a world-weary statue, tired of everything. Tired of gazing out into perfect light, the fountain, the tourists. Bored by his own face. His eyes show it. They have the glaze of marble, there is something dead in them—it is his only flaw. But as they speak even these eyes change, giving way. Correct themselves. Something there opens like a small, dark flower. "Les fleurs du mal," she says.

"Pourquoi tu as dit 'les fleurs du mal'?" he asks.

She shrugs. She has no idea. She hasn't been well.

One is consoled by his company. He stops—there is no doubt about it—this sad trajectory she is on.

He starts talking more quickly because she seems to be understanding. He changes tone and position and she senses he is saying something more urgent. At the end of it he says,

"Tu comprends?"

"Non."

"Ce n'est pas grave."

As always, her notebook is open.

He writes in it, "Ce soir, vendredi, Bambou, 10h30."


## 2


Their first meeting is the night of the day she first saw him in the dazzling light. Though it is dark, the fountain still flows. It will flow all night while the people of Vence sleep.

They have planned to meet at the Place du Grand Jardin in the center of town at the bar called the Bambou, next to La Régence. He is already there when she arrives and he is still beautiful.

"Salut," he says; he kisses her twice on the cheeks.

The planes of his face effortlessly take on the darkness. What happened in light does not occur now, but it is no less startling. He sits smoking under the small, white lights. He turns his passionate and mobile head slowly to survey the others at the bar. He speaks quickly and she has a difficult time understanding what he says. And when she speaks in her simple English he whispers slower, more slowly. They smile at not being able to understand each other. They are guests of this earth—not really at home here. It is easy to see. The waitress offers her a French/English dictionary. But what good would a dictionary do? Even now it is already too late. "Non," he says quickly. It would violate some unspoken agreement they have already entered. "Non."

He is alone, he says. He likes to be alone. "Je m'amuse." I amuse myself, he says. He's not sure why he's here. She has come to look. He too stares at her. She is in the center of her beauty.

He is alone. "Je m'amuse," he says.

They talk about film. She tells him her hero is Godard. He

tells her he loves Eric Rohmer. He tells her he likes Martin Scorsese, the director of New York.

"What do you do in New York?" he asks.

"Je suis écrivain."

He laughs. "Really? What do you write?"

"Stories."

"Ah oui? Toi? Les livres? Je ne le crois pas. Combien de livres?" He doesn't believe it. He makes a sarcastic French face.

"Deux."

"Deux livres? And they are published?"

"One is published. One will be out in the spring."

"Vraiment?" He doesn't believe a word she says. It doesn't really matter.

"You are in France to write another?"

"Oui."

He shakes his head. "I don't believe you."

"Ce n'est pas grave," she says.

"Is that what the cahier is for? To write down the book?"

"Oui."

He is reading Balzac, he tells her.

"What kind of book are you writing?"

"Un roman d'amour."

He smiles. He talks about Balzac. He is sarcastic with intelligence. Along with his beauty it makes him feel trapped. He lights another cigarette. He loves France. Anything French. Bizet, Sartre, Poulenc, Balzac. The tennis player Leconte. He's trying to tell her that the designer Kenzo is French.

"Non."

"Oui."

They laugh.

He pulls the hair back from his face. She wants him. She wants the man with the cheveux longs. They talk about odd things. Les compositeurs russes. Les peintres américains. He likes Jasper Johns. He does not like Edward Hopper. He likes Jackson Pollock.

He doesn't understand why she went to see Michael Jackson. "Mais Michael Jackson est mauvais," he says.

"Oui, mais j'aime Michael Jackson, beaucoup."

She lies the way all Americans lie, he says.

"Do you like Du-ka-keese?" he asks.

"Oui. I will vote for him. He will win."

He names American presidents. Ronald Reagan, Richard Nixon, Gerald Ford. "Why are American presidents always so stupid?" He liked Jimmy Carter. "Zhee-mee Car-tare was a good president. He was my favorite president."

"Oui?"

"Oui. He grows coconuts!" he says.

"No."

"Si."

"Non. He grows peanuts."

"Oui, c'est ça! Peanuts!"

He laughs.

He talks about the films of Coppola. "One is good and then one is terrible and then one is good again." He shrugs.

"Did you see the last film by Wim Wenders?" she asks him. "Bruno Ganz was an angel."

"Non."

We talk about actors.

"You reminded me when I saw you of the German actress who is très belle."

"Oui." I know who she is. "And you," she says, "it is as if you have stepped out of a film by Truffaut."

He laughs.

"What is your name?" she asks.

He hesitates a second and then, "Lucien," he says. "Et toi?"

"I am called Catherine."

They write all their names down in the cahier. He writes Lucien Marcel Stéphane Christian. She writes Catherine Stephanie Christine. "We have the same name," he says quietly.

He lights a cigarette. "Are you married?" he asks.

"Non."

"Mais pourquoi?"

"Je ne sais pas. Et toi?"

"Non," he says emphatically. "Non. The woman for me does not exist." She laughs, but he doesn't laugh.

They are at the limits of language and patience. It is zero o'clock, he says. He stares at her. It is time to go. "Tu viens?" he asks.

She wants the beautiful man with the cheveux longs.

They don't talk on the way back to the fountain. They're quiet and she feels the flow of their desire. She feels his hand moving through light. The moon spills on them like some dangerous liquid. He directs her silently to his apartment, across the street from the fountain. She feels his hands on her back. "Arrête," he says. He holds her gently from behind and guides her up a flight of stairs. "Arrête," he whispers.

It is that simple. He says, "Tu viens?"

She says, "Oui."

And in the room: "Viens. Viens, ici."

## 3

When I open my eyes I am shocked to see him next to me, sleeping. He stirs, opens his eyes for a moment, remembers, says nothing and we make love. There is no other solution.

Everything he does is beautiful.

Afterwards I look out his window onto a courtyard of flowers. He makes café. "So many flowers," I say. He bends me gently over the sill. The flowers waver. He holds me down.

"Tell me about les fleurs," he says, as he enters me. As everything opens. I tell him I can't believe all the roses in France. So many roses. Every variety. So many beautiful kinds. Such colors. Apricot, pale yellow. I tell him my sister's name is Rose.

"Oui, c'est vrai?"

I tell him I love the flowers of France. So many yellow roses.

"Rosebud," he says and looks at me knowingly. He smiles. I think of a young French boy in a dark theater watching *Citizen Kane* for the first time, now this man moving slowly, deeply inside.

Rosebud.

He puts what he calls French music on the record player. "Tu connais Jean-Luc Ponty?"

"Oui."

Next to his bed is a book by Balzac. On the back it says, "En 1829, il rève d'une femme passionnée fière et indouptée, qui serais subjugée par son amour."

It is true what he said the night before. He has no telephone. He does not like the telephone. He likes to be alone.

He dresses for work. I walk around the room. "It is very small," he says.

"It is not so small."

"Si," he says.

It's like the apartment in New York. No real kitchen, just appliances against the wall. A small fireplace.

The radio news in a dazzling French. I don't understand a word.

I remember the savage afternoon I tried to speak through.

Perrier in the refrigerator. Dishes in the sink. I wonder what he eats.

He has only a bed. No desk, no table, no bureau. He must do everything in his bed, I imagine. He is the French man of my fantasies. This beautiful man with the cheveux longs.

I know it's true: slowly he's dismissed everything. His family, his friends, his religion, his beliefs. And then his hopes. Until it is just he and Balzac in a room with a bed. Occasionally he'll bring a woman home.

He hands me a Perrier. I am drinking Perrier, I think, after making love with a French man in France. French music plays on the record player.

There's a copy of *Libération*, on the floor. I pick it up and open it. A headline says "La Mort Ordinaire de Raymond Carver." It says, "Le cancer l'a tué le 2 août à Port Angeles, près de Seattle, après une vie ravagée par l'alcool. Il racontait la vie des pauvres gens de l'Amérique avec un vocabulaire qui n'était pas plus riche qu'eux. C'était là tout l'art d'un des plus grands écrivains américains contemporains."

It seems all the more sad in French somehow.

There is a single, small cactus on his windowsill. "It's my cactus collection," he says. I am happy to understand a joke in French.

I pick up the Balzac and I try to read the beginning. "Tu ne comprends rien," he laughs. "Rien du tout."

"Oui," I say. "C'est vrai."

He asks me if I know the Swiss painter who paints "beaucoup de femmes, beaucoup de sexe, et de violence."

"Non."

He steps away now. Separates from me. He's not sure how I got here in the first place. He recalls, I imagine, yesterday by the fountain.

I look out the window at a pulsing red rose.

He must go to work.

I get out my notebook. It feels dangerous to him, whatever I write there. He can't begin to imagine. He doesn't try.

He kisses me once more in the privacy of the small apartment. "Encore," I say.

No, he must work.

Out in the light as he resumes his position next to the fountain, I realize he is too beautiful for almost everything. I write, "She doesn't know how he stands there all day. She doesn't know how he makes it down the street safely." He would laugh. "Everything is difficult for him." Maybe he would laugh.

# 4

Occasionally we still talk on the phone though neither of us can bear the sort of sorrow it brings up in us.

I tell her I am so brown she wouldn't recognize me, and this makes her cry. I tell her my hair is white now from the sun. She can't stop sobbing.

I tell her she would love it here. The French are obsessed with food and wine and film and history.

She says, "Maybe I am French." I tell her I am trying to improve my French but that it's difficult.

She says that she still loves me, though she knows I don't believe it. She waits for a response and when I say nothing the tears begin again.

Choisir is to choose.

She says now that she has stopped seeing the woman called Clover. That it didn't mean anything, and that I must believe her.

I feel the static rage of the afternoon.

I tell her I live in a stone house now. "The house we lived in together in New York was made of stone too I guess. For you," I say, "it had no windows or door. But while I was away somehow you found the way out. You should be happy," I say.

She says that the affair is over. I say, "I don't believe you." Something in me has stopped.

"Today," she says, "Coco chased a little gray mouse under a woodpile." They've gone to visit our friends in the country for the weekend. I too start to cry.

The imperfect tense is used when an action which began in the past was interrupted and remained incomplete.

Something in me stops.

She sounds very young to me from so far away. I picture her just a girl reading *Death in Venice* and taking notes. And one day I will love her.

## 5

Her American friends come to Vence and they walk around the back streets looking at the villas. There's an astounding blue sky and the sun is hot and bright. This makes them happy. They are Americans; they are dependent on the weather for their moods. I like them, their simplicity, how easily they are satisfied. Their kindness. We pass Sylvia's house. We hear her loud, cigarette voice. "Oh, as a child I was *mad* about Mars! And then I learned that Mars was too cold! And Venus was too hot! And you couldn't put a foot straight on Mars and oh what a *bore!*"

I smile. I am growing very fond of Sylvia too, oddly attached to her—Sylvia who is never satisfied. I think of Allan, the Australian, sitting next to her and looking distraught.

"We never see enough of the moon! I mean the *real* moon! Or the photographs that came back from Mars! I want to see the real thing! Well, we've had enough science fiction."

My American friends laugh. They tell me the next space shuttle will be going up soon. They tell me in America they've invented a smokeless, odorless cigarette. I think how appalled Sylvia would be by this. To me the news seems from a place as distant as Mars. I try to hold my country in my mind.

I don't tell them that I have talked to her. I don't tell them about the man with the cheveux longs. I wouldn't know what to say.

I take them to the piscine municipale where I still go almost every day. I count white tiles, rafts, children. My friends tell funny stories about learning to swim. They remember Coney Island, Jones Beach—names I haven't heard in a long time. This year those beaches have been closed.

She seems so strange here, so out of place. Taller than the French and with that American je ne sais quoi—sitting at the bar high above the piscine. She is drinking menthe verte— I cross that out—she is drinking a pastis, no a Campari and soda, a whiskey, a vin blanc. She is softly humming to herself: an American love song, maybe. I am making her up as I go along. She is dreaming of a man with long hair. They meet at the bar every night before making love.

I watch the girls at poolside laughing and talking. Another girl, off alone, reads a book. She writes something down, then gets up and goes into the water. She still has braces. She is a virgin yet.

I think of Picasso's Marie-Thérèse, a girl of seventeen. She was interested in *nothing but sports*, Sylvia said, but she haunted his existence.

My American friends talk on and on like the French girls. I stare into the amorphous water shaped by the tile rectangle of pool. I am forced again to fully imagine what life will be like without her. Without those boundaries, without that shape. I cry. Nothing in this radiant day can console.

Tenir is to hold. Oublier is to forget.

I've been pretty good, they think; it's the first time I've cried all day. I take out my French book. Nicholas is lost.

At night we walk to dinner under a full moon. It's a year of thirteen moons, I tell them sadly. Unlike Sylvia I have never wanted to see pictures of it. It's Friday night and all the French are out smoking cigarettes, talking, kissing each other, once, twice on the cheeks. Incredible ice creams float by. Many-colored drinks in the warm fluent evening. Our waitress at Le Pêcheur du Soleil has a large polka dotted bow in her hair and a high singing voice that makes you think any moment she might fly away.

We watch the people pass. "There is a certain type of French man," I tell them. "Long brown hair, great nose, dark sweater, cigarettes, a moody, brooding expression, carrying a book of poetry or philosophy under his arm. You can find him in every small French town," I say. "I love that man."

I open my notebook. I guess I'm still thinking that this handful of words might save me. I think of the two of them—the American woman, the French man—and imagine there might be a way for them to live.

There's a warm breeze on this moonlit night and somehow

I know it is the middle of my life. It is the middle of August and I am deep inside a village in France, having given myself up entirely to it for the summer. I am surrounded by the thick walls of this ancient city.

Strangely I think I will look back on these days as among the happiest in my life.

I order a pizza called Vendredi.

## 6

They sit at the bar and listen to the sad songs on the yearning French radio. Again, someone leaves someone else. I know it happens to almost everyone.

"You have beautiful hair," she tells him.

"Non. C'est normal."

His hair is longer than hers was when she left. She had promised to grow it.

He smokes a cigarette. Even though it's night, it is as hot as the day. "I saw you writing in your notebook and crying today. Why were you crying?"

"Parce que . . . I can't explain."

"Look," I say. "Over there at that table."

"Oui?"

"That man—he is about to leave the woman for someone else. She does not know it, but she will never see him again." I take a cigarette from his package. "There would be no use in looking for him. She could never find him. He is going far away." Lucien looks at me strangely. I put my head down on the marble table.

"How do you know that?"

I shrug. "It's hard for me to always speak French," I say.

"But this is France," he says in French. "Americans think all the world should speak English." He does not want to go to America, he says. "Jamais. L'Amérique du Sud, oui, mais pas l'Amérique du Nord. Pas les États-Unis."

"Not New York?"

"Never New York."

It is foolish to believe that because we do not have much language that we cannot hurt one another.

We make a list of the places we would like to go. He writes Afrique, Portugal, Mexique, Australie. I write Sweden, Greece. "I would like to go to the Corse Arturo Toscanini en Italie," I tell him. I write Italy. I write the Hotel Gustav Mahler. "It is in Paris," I say. "I would like to go there too." I write next 7 Place Antony-Mars. He laughs again.

"I can take you there," he says.

"Oui."

"It is near the cemetery."

At the bar where they meet before making love they amuse themselves. He draws a map of the world on the marble table. He asks her to label the countries. To prove to him that Americans know more than where the United States is.

He asks me to name the Benelux countries and to show him where they are.

He asks me what I do for work. "Like her," I say and I point to my favorite waitress. "What is the word?"

"Une serveuse."

"Oui, une serveuse."

"Tu travailles maintenant?"

"Non."

We make a list of our favorite films on a napkin. I write *Breathless, Last Year at Marienbad, Lacombe, Lucien*. "Lucien," I say, "Comme toi." He smiles. He writes Eric Rohmer.

All of his films?

"Oui."

He writes *Chinatown, Raging Bull, Citizen Kane*.

"Rosebud." I say. He smiles.

I write *The Conformist, The Marriage of Maria Braun, Jules et Jim*. He writes *The Godfather, Blue Velvet*.

He says he doesn't like Meryl Streep. "Have you seen the American movie *9½ Weeks*?" This makes me laugh.

— 82 —

"Yes."

"Kim Basinger." He likes her. "And Mickey Rourke."

We talk about the Germans. Fassbinder. Schlondorf. Wenders. "You should see the new Wim Wenders movie," I tell him. "Bruno Ganz is an angel."

He tells me that from the start I've reminded him of the actress he loves most. German. Très belle.

"And you. Out of an unmade film by the dead Truffaut."

And so we are lovers.

On the way to his house I practice my French, pointing to things in shop windows. "La robe. La poupée. La couteau."

"*Le* couteau."

"Le couteau. Les gants. Le parapluie. Le suntan lotion. What is the word for 'suntan lotion'?"

"L'huile solaire."

"Oui. L'huile solaire. Chauve-souris," she says, pointing to the sky. Bats.

Suddenly the night is unaccountably dark. What is the word, I want to know, for "dark"?

He smiles. I open my notebook. In the night when he sleeps he is afraid of something, I write.


## 7


He feels the need to tell me that he is not normal. He is méchant. Un peu violent. Un peu étrange.

"Yes, I know," I tell him.

He doesn't believe me.

He tells me he writes letters to people, puts them in envelopes, puts on the stamps, but he never sends them. He does not write for anyone else. He writes for himself—to understand himself.

He tells me he has une amie. "Avec un *e*." A woman. He says he loves her beaucoup.

"Oui, je comprends. Ce n'est pas grave," I tell him.

He doesn't believe me. He doesn't want to talk about her. He just wants me to know that she exists, that he is not available.

He hopes he does not hurt me by telling me about the other woman. He is not really méchant at all, I think. He feels shame, he tells me. He writes "honte" in my notebook. I remember that word from once before.

I show him some photographs I have taken. He tries to see Vence through my eyes. He smiles at the "Votez Mitterand" graffiti. He looks at pictures of the marché, the cathédrale, photos of Nice, of Arles, of a dark woman walking next to the Rhône. He puts them back in the envelopes. "Je déteste les photos," he says. He says something about privacy. "Never take my photo," he says.

He thinks photographs are death. There is no changing his mind.

I show him a boy at another table who has the potential of being a younger, blonder, less spectacular Lucien, and he says, "Yes, but who would want that?"

"Many things," he says, "are difficult for me."

His father asks him to think seriously about something. But he is gravely misunderstood. With Lucien, everything is serious.

"Tell me more about your life."

He shrugs. There is nothing really to tell. "It is difficult for me."

"Oui, je comprends."

He reads *Libération*. He never reads *Nice-Matin* or *Paris-Match*. Jamais. He's not sure what to make of me. I seem silly. Were it not for all the crying, were it not for the deux livres.

He wants to tell me he's like smoke. All the world is smoke, I want to tell him. All the world disappears. Look how the olive trees dissolve with tears, I would like to say.

"You cry too much. C'est trop."

She begged me to turn away. Not to look at that red road. But I looked anyway. Because as hard as I try, I do not know how to look away.

He's also saying you drink too much. In France women don't sit at a table in the center of town in the middle of the day and drink three, four pastis. He wants to know "Why are you alone? Why are you not married?"

His hair is longer than hers was when I left.

He doesn't trust her. He says he does not like Americans. Americans do not like les bêtes. Do not like pets. He will never understand important things about America. He will never understand that many of us are ashamed of Ronald Reagan. He does not like Americans because of Star Wars, because of our stupidity and arrogance. "Americans do not know their geography. Americans have no history." We do not like ourselves sometimes, I'd like to tell him. Not like the French who seem to love every single thing about themselves.

"I hear there are fascists here in the south of France," I say.

He laughs. "It is a very small percentage," he says. "It is not a problem."

One gets tired of the French, their chauvinism, their fussy dogs. All the small birds they roasted.

"Tell me about working at the galerie."

"There is nothing to tell."

I don't know how to begin to ask him what I want to know.

"I do not write or paint like you and your friends in America," he says. "I only make money from those who write and paint." He says all this as the grandes têtes pass—enormous puppets with huge heads. It's some saint's day. He laughs cynically, and then he is silent.

She is so taken with him that even these enormous puppet heads do not intrude. He's had to talk louder to be heard over all the commotion that I'm only now just noticing, as he lights a last cigarette at the bar. Small bits of colored paper shower us. The word in English. I'm trying to think of the word—confetti. Confetti floats between them.

He writes in my notebook: "Minuit ½, besoin de position

horizontale, lit, tu viens?"

He writes:

"Pourquoi? Pour rien."

He writes:

"Pourqui? Pour moi."

He writes:

"Après? Rien."

"Je comprends," I write.

They walk. She touches the beautiful forever of his face. His passive, indifferent head.

He is intensely private. He seems a little startled that suddenly I'm in his apartment. That somehow he has asked me back here again.

He folds over the pillow and puts it under my lower back. I am raised toward him and he lowers his magnificent head to me and we meet each other halfway. His long hair is draped over my swollen belly.

"Sel de mer," he says.

"Oui. I am salty. Soon there will be blood."

This excites him. We imagine together the blood that is to come. I tell him a story about the ruby jewels hidden deep within the kingdom.

He smiles. He turns over on his stomach to sleep. "I wish you could see your back," I say.

"Comment?"

"Nothing."

It is a beautiful back. It is a back like hers.

This was the truth she said: We would always be together. Everything would be OK. All she ever wanted was me. I see now that the truth is something that shifts and changes. The truth is not really the truth. That is all. I'm drifting off. Alors—

I remember her lying on the bed. Her arms pinned behind her like wings.

He speaks French in his sleep. "Le feu," he says. Fire.

At night, when he sleeps, he is afraid of something.

## 8

"You!" she bellows. "You have become an absolute stranger!"

I realize that it is true I have not seen Sylvia in many days. Right away she makes it clear that this will simply not do. "Do tell me something," she says. "A story."

She says it was a mad thing to do. "You and thieves!" She says she would have taken me to Michael Jackson. I laugh picturing Sylvia in her beat-up Citroën going anywhere. Sylvia at Michael Jackson! But she is serious.

"You say oui to *everything*! You think because they speak another language they are harmless.

"How did you say they steal the tickets?

"Oh, I suppose the Citroën might not have made it. But really! You know these mechanics. . . . Monica always believed in the garage completely until *everything fell apart*. These Citroëns are rather good cars, but the French don't have a *clue* how to fix them."

There's a knock at the door. "Yes, who is it?"

"It's me Miss Byrd, it's Allan."

"Yes, Allan, what can I do for you?"

"Well it's just that I noticed that you and the Hartgers and Marie hadn't gotten in when I passed by last night and it was late, so I just thought I'd stop by and see if you were all right."

"Yes, we're all right Allan. What did you think? That the four of us had died *simultaneously*?"

He laughs.

"Thank you all the same, Allan."

"Good-bye, Miss Byrd."

"Mustn't pay too much attention to Allan.

"Oh, it was different when Monica was alive. People let us live more. I never had a thought that I'd survive her. After thirty years one simply *forgets* that it's possible.

"You know she could never find a thing. Books, papers, clothing. She had a very intricate filing system, but, well, it simply didn't work. I'm still getting her things in order.

Packing away her winter clothes. You know she was very spoiled as a child, but not in any of the ways that really matter.

"Royalty, my Monica. And a very great beauty. Here's a picture of her. Isn't she lovely?

"Oh we had loads of fun. Here we are in Tunisia. Here we are back by the geraniums."

Lola writes saying that I should come home. She writes asking how long I think I can keep running away from the real world.

Long, I think. A long time. Besides, this is the real world now. Sylvia. The butcher. The baker. I think of the olive man in the marché. The olives d'ail I buy every Friday. The chèvre, the capers and anchovies, the fresh eggs. I think of the French I'm beginning to really learn. I think of Perrier.

I think of his slow mouth.

I think of him saying "Slowly." "More slowly." And, "Qu'est-ce que tu as dit?"

I remember the summers it was so hot all we could do was drink. Me trying to write, and Lola with some terrible job. The air conditioner broken. Still it was not all bad. We loved each other. We had fun, I think. It was a different New York then. CBGB. Patti Smith. Joie de Vivre. No deadly disease.

"I'm thinking of writing a sonnet to Monica," Sylvia says. "I think it would be a good way to begin my life as a poet." I smile. She is talking against the same field of geraniums where they once stood together.

Lola writes that despite everything, she loves only me, wants only me. I think of the stone house she lived in all those years without windows or doors.

This time, Lola, I let you go. This time I set us free.

I recite part of a poem a young poet once told me:

> Love is a shadow
> How you cry after it
> Listen: there are its hooves, it has
> gone off like a horse.

is a petit pastis.

in and orders a Coca-Cola with

st ça," I say. I am getting sillier and
ie.

er a song in English:

, row, row your boat,
tly down the stream
rrily, merrily, merrily, merrily
e is but a dream.

e it into French. I row in the air with my

eautiful young man broods. It's impossible to
e, even for a moment. He doesn't know why I
Or why I cry.
e is laughing. The American smokes Camel
u'est-ce que c'est le mot for 'camel'?" I ask,
e package. "Chameau," Jean says. "Et chamelle
du chameau."
ks sings on the radio, Tom Petty, "You don't
like a refugee."
his love of interiors and smoke? I look into the
at him and recognize myself there. It is like look-
ater. We reflect each other's solitude. I am not re-
n the bar. I am out there with him.
her man that works in the galerie talks to others,
s friends, feels a part of things. But not Lucien. I
m. I know him well. I will teach him my song. He
acefully through space alone.

## 11

ey imagine roses swollen with rain. And a white horse.
ey imagine opening the shutters on a world of extraordi-

---

"That's Sylvia Plath, Sylvia."
"Poor, darling Sylvia," she says, and takes my hand.

## 9

The woman is sitting at the bar, wearing her Chinese hat,
holding a notebook and crying.

She opens the letter again. "Stop running away," it says.
"Come back to your real life." A writer's real life is when and
where she is writing, she thinks. She is not running away in
these pages, she is running forward, embracing her real life.

In the book it will say, "The dark woman was cowardly
and always looked for her real life somewhere outside."

He appears from the old city. He's on his afternoon break.
"You cry too much," he says, and he just watches her cry. He
does not ask why and he doesn't offer comfort. He understands this: that it is not possible to say one word that would
make a difference. He just sits and watches her.

He's about to get up and leave.

"Attends," she says.

"La femme qui pleure," he says with bitterness. "Stop crying."

When she finally looks at him he seems to glow. How
beautiful he is at midday. The galerie closed. They listen to
American love songs on the French radio.

He says good. He says when she's not crying she looks like
the most beautiful actress, the German. It's what immediately
attracted him, he says, of course.

"Of course," she smiles "Et pourquoi pas?"

"You are always writing in that cahier," he says.

"Oui," I say. "C'est vrai."

"What are you writing?" he asks.

"I told you," I say, "un roman."

"Yes, but what does it say?"

I smile. We watch people pass. I feel a little happier. "Look," I say. "Over there." I point to a woman carrying presents and walking a poodle. "She has a dress shop in Cagnes-sur-Mer. Or maybe a salon-de-thé. Elle s'appelle Isabelle, non, Delphine."

He laughs. He realizes I have the power to change what he sees. He stares at me, asserting his own kind of power.

"I want the man with the cheveux longs," I say.

"You always want that man," he says.

"Oui."

We hurry to his apartment during the midday break. Every time she sees the roses she's shocked.

"Rosebud," he whispers.

"Speak English to me."

"Non. Speak French," he says. He caresses her foot. He sees he's got the power to take my words away, the thing he thinks I value most, and he likes that some days.

He's mistaken if he thinks he's not part of her real life now.

He sucks his middle finger. She watches. She has no underwear on; he knows that. He presses his finger to her beating— "Rosebud," he says.

Afterwards he looks at the small bruises he's left on her upper arms simply by touching them. He believes it is the only mark he leaves until he opens the notebook.


10

She goes to the Bar Marseillais across the street from the galerie where she can watch him work. He stands there in the impossible light in the raging, silent afternoon, next to rows and rows of art postcards. Sometimes he drinks from the fountain, sometimes he runs his beautiful hands under that liquid light. He puts a bottle under the mouth of the foun-

tain. He ho

Som

wind

book.

Stares

watches

of the blu

difficult fo

I would t

I write in my

*L'Intelligence a*

She drinks a

beginning to kno

years.

"Are you allema

"Non. Américaine

He likes American

don't you like the Eng

"Parce que les anglai

English burned Joan of A

I laugh. Maybe I've had

His name is Jean too. He

He is monégasque. He says

tional. He points to each pers

Monégasque et une jeune amér

He's noticed the notebook too

for?"

"I am writing a novel."

"What type?"

"A love story. It takes place in Fra

are beautiful flowers, and so much lig

fountain, a woman who weeps."

He nods. "Will the Bar International b

"Peut-être."

I learn strange things here. That Perrier

ears curl and then you are morte. But is tha

could be saying?

I learn that a momie

An American comes

lemon. "Coca-Cola c'e

sillier with each mom

I teach the barten

Row

Ger

Me

Lif

I try to translat

arms. We laugh.

Outside the b

forget he is ther

drink so much.

But today sh

cigarettes. "Q

pointing to th

est la femme

Stevie Nic

have to live

What is

mirror out

ing into w

ally here

The ot

jokes, ha

know hi

rows gi

"Th

Th

nary heat and light. A courtyard of roses."

"More slowly," he says.

"In the courtyard there is a beautiful gardener. What is 'gardener' in French, Lucien?"

"Jardinier."

I tell him a story, half in English, half in French.

"Franglais," he says, wincing.

"The jardinier lives near the cemetery," I say "He grows the flowers they put in the glass globes."

He smiles.

"One day," I say, "he decides to sail around the world. He is looking for water lilies. He is looking for the sea rose of his dreams. He observes the clouds. He is guided by stars. His long hair blows in the wind.

"It is not really so hard to imagine. Much of his life he's spent looking out at water, on one beautiful coast or another. He will smell salt, catch fish, hold a green anchor in his hands. He will re-name the world. For once he will understand something about his life."

Lucien shakes his head no.

"He will."

"Non," he says quietly.

"He calls each island a flower: Tulipe, Rosier à Cent Feuilles, Pensées. A few names from the old world he keeps: Greenland maybe, perhaps Finland. France."

He smiles.

"Maybe there is some hope for the man from the most beautiful coast."

"Oui," he says. "Peut-être."

"And all night long he dreams of the sea rose. And the Red Sea."

"But he is afraid of water," he says.

"Non," she laughs. "A sailor who fears water?"

"Yes. Of course. It's not unusual. It's very common. Why the Red Sea?"

"No reason," she says. "It's just what he dreams. One day he meets a mermaid."

"Quoi?"

"A mermaid."

"What are you saying? Explain."

"A woman with the tail of a fish."

"I think you are very crazy," he says in English.

"The mermaid loves him at first sight. Her French is not good, but good enough to say, 'Je t'adore.' She knows a few other words: ascenseur, ouvrez la porte, l'explorateur."

He laughs. I close my eyes. "And their lovemaking. It's like nothing else in this world.

"During the day he explains to her what flowers are, he describes gardens. And a movie called *Citizen Kane*. Together at night on the sea they dream of rosebuds. Day after day, night after night, they float together in their watery globe.

"Now and then he'll return to the place he was born—the most beautiful coast in the world. But he always goes back to the sea. He misses her too much. And she can never live on land."

## 12

Dear Lola,

I sit alone under a red and white umbrella at eleven o'clock at night. It's still warm. In the air you can hear every conceivable language. I'm under an umbrella that says "Jupiter, Bière Belge." My God, where am I?

I am alone tonight and I am drunk. And I am writing (the people at the other tables stare) a strange little book.

I stare back looking at the fantastic noses of the French. These noses aren't at every table but at some tables and sometimes at La Régence, and certainly on the man with the cheveux longs.

Deux ou trois vin rouges at twenty-three hours is different though than deux ou trois at fourteen o'clock in the afternoon. Americans drink too much, Lucien says. What he means is American women.

The Arab women are busy at work. They come and kiss me on the cheeks. They are a little worried about me. They say this in French.

You looked very beautiful that weekend you were so sad. We fought and fought and then made love. We blamed it afterwards on the grappa.

I'm sorry. There should have been more room for kindness.

It feels late to me but here all les enfants are still awake. Why do the French never go to sleep?

I am a woman alone drinking vin rouge while the French at every other table eat.

It's true that often I felt alone even when I was with you. Not your fault.

A small French boy holds his small French penis. He is barefoot. His parents mangent bien. I think he's the same boy I saw at the pool today.

It's a little odd sitting under a large umbrella in the middle of the night.

Lola, they never get tired of throwing each other into the pool.

The little boy is sleepy but well-behaved. He's tired of playing. He's tired of everything there is to do here.

A man passes with a T-shirt that says NO TIME TO WASTE in English.

I'm writing night and day now. I'm trying not to waste anything.

Ooh là là. Lola, là, là. Lo. La.

The French woman, the one who's friends with the Arab women, comes and sits next to me. She'd like me to go home with her.

And the man with the NO TIME TO WASTE T-shirt (on front and on back) circles like some moving billboard, like a man in a film or a dream. But I never have dreams like that.

At night I try to dream us back together. But I can't see us anymore. It's getting so dark.

I do not know if she is beautiful, I write.

I'll never send it.

Lola, I still love you.


## 13


"It is a real pain the way you're always carrying around that notebook. Like a photographer, taking everything. I don't believe in it."

"Don't be superstitious," I tell him. "I can never get it down that right. You've no need to worry."

She remembers now telling Lola in some detail about the woman she would come to love.

"You invade my privacy. The French are very private. Not like the Americans."

She remembers the story she once wrote about her older brother, dying, in a white room. She was only a child then.

"You have an American shirt on," I tell him. "Many Americans wear that shirt."

"La Coste," he says. "Don't be ridiculous. La Coste is French. What's wrong with you anyway?"

"I don't know anymore." I point to his shirt. "What is the word for 'alligator' in French?"

"It's a crocodile, not an alligator."

"What is the word for 'crocodile'?"

"Crocodile." He smiles.

"What is that sound?"

"Les pompiers," he says.

I say, "Le Bal des Pompiers."

"Stop talking nonsense," he says.

"I will be one of your stories," he says. "I'll expect to read about all of this one day. In the book you are writing how will you describe me?"

"You will never recognize yourself."

"I don't believe you. You invade my privacy."

He's unhappy every time he sees his name in my note-book. He writes things like "pas bon" next to each entry.

"What will it say in the book?" he asks as she takes his shirt with the alligator off.

"It will say, once there was a man with cheveux longs who lived alone on the edge of an ancient city. He was moody and beautiful and solitary but sometimes he took women that he saw on the street home to bed with him."

"Ce n'est pas intéressant," he says. "Ce n'est pas bon," he says as he moves into me, disappears into me.

"What will it say in the book?"

That he tried to save her, I think to myself, but he could not.

"La Coste," I say.

"Non."

"Cheveux longs."

"Non."

Later he writes "fin" in my cahier. "That stands for 'The End' in French," he says.

## 14

He's not sure why she's here. He takes her notebook. All he knows is she is writing a book and he does not want to be the subject of it. He writes about the hero: "Et maintenant le héros, maître de son destin, prend une décision existentielle, disparaissant des pages du livre, échappant des mains sataniques de l'écrivain avec un rire méprisant. Voilà. C'est fait. Imaginez le désarrois de l'auteur, soudain face à une oeuvre vide de son cœur."

He writes, "Fin."

Just because you write that doesn't mean it's the end.

There's an excess of feeling today. Excess of heat and bees.

It's the lunch hour. He gets up. Closes the shutters. "In my country this heat would be called 100 degrees," I tell him.

He reads: "She felt like a fruit being split open by this man from the south who had lived a long time among flowers and fruit. She was that ripe, she thought. He licked the juice like a hungry child. Today he cannot get enough. There was such sweetness there."

He reads: "In the agony of her body he tries to speak, but she covers his mouth. They walk on some shattering, dazzling edge."

Imagining the end, there is an excess of passion. A strange attachment.

He does not like what I write in that book. He says he is méchant. He tries to explain. He makes up women all the time. He is alone and he likes that. There are letters he never sends.

I write in my notebook: "He wants to bring her to a wordless place."

"In English," he asks, "what is the word for 'boîtes aux lettres'?"

"Mailbox."

"Oui. Mailbox."

He's méchant, violent, not to be trusted.

"You have invented me—this man with the cheveux longs. It's very evident. I represent your surrender."

I smile. It's a warning I refuse to heed. He's writing me letters he'll never send. He's told me in advance. "Yes, but haven't we all invented each other? And ourselves? What selves we have?"

"Speak French."

He sees lovers everywhere in the street because this is after all France, but he doesn't know what to make of it. He says he does not, cannot believe in them.

He reads: "His eyes are like night without day."

"Non," he says. "Tu es folle."

"Shh—" I say. "One must take great care in a foreign country."

"Yes," he says bored. "You have come here to die. It's evident," he says in French. "It's very clear."

I laugh.

"It's normal—to travel somewhere."

They walk past the cemetery. They walk up the stairs of the small house in France. "What is the word for—" She's forgetting the meanings. At the door he hesitates. Shakes his head. Looks at her hopelessly.

She feels wounded by the brutal planes of his face in the hallway light.

He presses her against the door. He does not like what she writes in that book.

"Qu'est-ce que tu veux?" she whispers.

"Stop telling me stories," he says. "That's what I want."

He wants to bring her to a wordless place. Where she puts down her cahier.

"What do you want from me?" she asks.

"Say nothing now." He covers her mouth for a minute.

They enter the small room. "What do you want?"

He does not know.

She recalls the edge of the dazzling, the dangerous—

He bends her over the white bed in the small room. "Non." He stops. She gives out a small cry. She turns over, lifts her skirt, feels the bluntness of her desire slowly sharpen. She presses herself on to him.

"Don't look at me that way," she thinks he says. "Arrête."

She forces him to the floor. "What do you want from me?" she asks.

"Tout." He laughs. "Rien."

He enters her hard. "Harder," she says. He splits her in two and then further. She says, "Break me."

"Speak French," he says. "Non." He changes his mind. "Say nothing. Say nothing or I will stop."

"Never stop," she says.

"Arrête," he whispers.

"Arrête," she says back. "Arrête."

He holds still in her. "Don't move," he says.

She laughs wildly. It is laughter of the mentally ill. She's heard it before. "Stop then," she says to herself. The laughter of someone newly jailed.

"You said arrête," he says sarcastically. "I heard you say arrête."

"Don't stop." She moves and he begins to move. Now with great inevitability. With great, deep, slow—never stop.

In the agony of her body he tries to speak, but she covers his mouth. They walk on some shattering, some dazzling edge. Far away. He bites down.

"Lucien!" she calls out. She is saying his name. He laughs.

"Lucien," she says again and again, the only syllables left in the world. It is as he wanted it. Then nothing. As he wanted it.

When they're conscious again, they laugh. She tries to catch her breath. "My God," she says. She rests her hand on his back.

"Only touch is not a lie," she whispers to him. "Only touch."

"Non," he says, "you are wrong." He looks at her gravely. "Touch, too, is a terrible lie."


## 15

Today Sylvia insists she read my tarot cards.

Must I know the future? I wonder.

"Oh, it's not like *that*! But I *am* curious to see what's happening with you! Strange girl, you are. You and that notebook. I must say I quite admire it.

"I could barely take a step without Monica. I thought it wouldn't be possible. But, well, I've managed. Foolish me!

"Go ahead and shuffle then," she says.

I shuffle the deck, pick the Ten of Cups, the World, the Lover, the King of Wands.

"Charmed one!" she exclaims.

But then, darkness. I pick the Eight of Swords, the Tower, the Wheel of Fortune, the Death card.

I see a woman turning away. A woman standing on a shore looking out over water. A woman blindfolded.

There's a preponderance of swords.

"You are taking stock," she says. "I'm afraid the breakup is essential to your movement in the world. There is great change in store.

"Someone from the past keeps returning. It's sad. Well quite sad. The whole world is opening up to you but there is a turning away from love here that is necessary in order for you to take your own journey. More things will be possible now. You are breaking away from certain emotional bonds and restrictions. But it is painful, my dear. It's in this card— which shows you bound to the earth, closed up, filled with indecision, the inability to move.

"But you are moving nonetheless. Look here. There's a reappraisal going on. You are making peace with the swords through a kind of death."

I look at the pictures curious that they still stand for something to someone. To Sylvia—at her age. I guess I'm glad it's still possible to make some connections. Maybe we're not so terribly alone. Each object. "Strange one." "Stranger," they all say.

"And, oh my! It's possible you're going to fall in love with a fire sign. An Aries or a Leo!" She laughs. "All this—

"It's the beginning of your time, Catherine. There is much expansion here—in your person, your spirit. You are a moving soul. Oh I quite like that, a moving soul in the universe, a life in transit. You are looking at it all and in your vast wisdom you contemplate, take stock and then continue.

"There will be money from an artistic endeavor.

"There will be prosperity, dear one, and happiness."

A plane flies by dropping fire retardant. He tells me about the time the hills above Nice caught fire. Smoke filling the city. The Americans still walking along the Promenade des Anglais, still on the beach, while his country goes up in flames. "It is the way of the Americans."

"I'm tired," I say. I'm getting tired of this.

He tells me other things he does not like about Americans. La guerre. Star Wars. "Americans," he says, have "pas de goût." No taste. He says Ronald Reagan.

"Je déteste Ronald Reagan," I tell him. "Et George Bush." I shake my head.

"Yes, but he will win. Regarde," he says. "Le sondage." Polls say he is ahead now. He is smiling.

"It is no joke, Lucien." I can't figure out how Bush got ahead. Where have I been?

I want to tell him, describe to him what it's like for me, an American, to be in France for the first time.

I tell him about the first time I stood on a balcony here and opened the shutters. What it felt like.

He's wondering how I can afford to just stay here in France; I must be very rich, as he believes all Americans are.

"No." I try to explain. "I have won a prize."

"Comme le Lotto?"

"Pas exactement." I try to explain to him that I have won a prize that originated "pendant l'administration de JFK pour les artistes." I'm not sure he's understanding any of it. "Its name is" and I say it in English.

She knows she's speaking English like a foreign language. She's forgetting the meanings.

He says it is something good about America—a prize like that. "Have you been to Californie?" he asks me. It is another good thing he has heard about America.

"Yes," I tell him. "One time. San Francisco. It is like this part of France."

"Oui, bien sûr, that is why it is so good," he laughs. He

loves when he can make a joke with me.

"France is better," he says. I tell him he is right.

"France is better. Intellectuals and artists in my country have no hope. Only the people who make the money. I'm tired," she says.

"Yes, but there is the prize," he says. "Don't be so stupid."

He would like to hurt her a little because despite everything, despite himself, he is growing to like her and she is an American and he wants nothing to do with Americans. So he picks an impossible subject to talk about just to remind himself that there's no real talking to her. He talks about the latest French discovery: a scientist has found that water has a memory. Next he talks about Wittgenstein.

She has read the *Investigations*, she tells him.

He makes one of those sarcastic French expressions, and she knows he is impressed. But it doesn't really matter, the conversation can go no further.

He asks her why she wants to be in France. Pourquoi?

She tells him there is no place for her in America anymore. She says the phone rings too much there. She says there is no hope. She tells him that it is very beautiful here. And also it is good to be in a country where every child can speak the language better than she can.

She said: love.

She said: forever.

"What did you expect?" he asks.

Letters from home talk about the intense, the frightening heat. The greenhouse effect. The polluted beaches. One fish dinner a week.

I tell him in my country it's 105 degrees. Every day. That's 40 degrees centigrade.

He says he doesn't understand why the whole world isn't on the metric system.

I say I don't want to talk about that. It's boring.

He shrugs.

It occurs to her that it's possible that the idea of the beautiful stranger is more interesting than the stranger himself.

I open the paper. I picture the future election of George Bush this moody young man predicts so casually. It will not surprise me I think. It will be just another in a series of betrayals and disappointments.

I think I'd like to tell him the story about riding on the American highway. An autoroute. There had been an accident and cars were backed up for a long way. The street was black. It was summer. We thought it was the terrible glare, but it wasn't. It was the blood of cows. Livers, hearts. Hooves and heads. I was sure I was looking at our life together. It was the shape our pain had taken. And Lola kept saying, don't look, don't look. But of course I did. We were never the same after that.

But I don't tell it. I don't have the strength to find the French. "George Bush," I say shaking my head. America. My poor, doomed country.

Sometimes I refuse to speak French and he refuses to speak English and we just sit there like that. He thinks I'm childlike, holding my schoolgirl cahier all the time.

She orders her third, maybe her fourth drink.

"Bateau ivre," he says, pointing at her.

"Rimbaud," she says.

"He is the typique français," I say, writing it down, "with his jambon and pâté, with his cigarettes and moto."

"Don't write that in your notebook," he says.

"I am not writing about you."

"You lie," he says in French.

He refuses to speak English. She refuses to speak French. She can't tell him about the cows in the road. The shape her misery took.

She climbs on top of him. She groans with sadness and pleasure. She's moaning; he knows what that means.

He wants to know all about her lover, the one she cries for in her sleep, but he can't ask. He doesn't know how to ask for anything.

He just wants her to know that the woman for him does not exist. She realizes now that the other woman he told her about, the amie avec un *e*, does not exist either. She will never appear.

He thinks she is vain. With her handful of photos, her French man from a film, her mirror, lipsticks, her *image*.

She knows she can make him fall in love with her. It's part of her arrogance that she can have anything she wants and she picks him. She knows he knows it. And he doesn't have the will to do anything about it.

He remembers the times he used to take drinks from the fountain. The time before he looked up. He's nostalgic for the time he was innocent of her. This foolish American, who weeps.

"Listen," she says. "I am the fountain you drink from. I am the water you would die without." She smiles. "Remember," she says, "how hot it can get."

He laughs suddenly. And she laughs. It is not, they guess, all that terrible.

She is his first American, he tells her and he puts his head in his hands, feigning exasperation.

"Non."

"Si."

"Non."

"OK, you are not my first."

The dream last night was about who would get the TV. Who would get which records, which books. I suppose I'll have to give back her *Death in Venice*.

What a stupid dream, I think. Who cares who gets the TV?

He asks why she's written "lesbian desire" in her notebook.

She shrugs.

She simply wants to hear that he loved somebody once. It would make her feel better. But he can't say what she wants to hear.

She's une femme inconnue. The woman in the Chinese hat.

In bed she asks him to take her far away. She says she wants to go far. Loin.

"You already are far away," he says. "How far do you

want to go?"

"Plus loin," she says. "More far. Farther."

## 17

She clings to his peripheral vision at the Bar Marseillais, at
the edge of the town where he stands faithfully so many
hours a day. Suddenly she disappears into the old city and he
excuses himself from work, follows her. But she's hard to
find. As she's turning into the boulangerie he is going into
the casino. They are really only a few yards away and they
feel each other in a sort of blind stupor, but they can't find
each other's bodies and they are lovers after all and need
this. She licks the sugar on the top of her brioche. Turns. He
is not there. But he is close. Closer. She sucks on her fingers
to call him forth. It is easy to get lost in such heat and light.

She wakes and sees that he is there next to her. She will
never get over the shock of seeing him first thing at the beginning of a day. He is beautiful and sleepy.

"I had a dream that I could not find you," he says. He caresses her.

"I had the same dream," she says and she weeps. He lets
her weep.

They make love. Then he gets up for work.

"Pas encore," I say. "Not yet."

"Oui."

She tells him more about the dream. "They kiss once,
twice, on the cheeks, a formality, and also a way of saying
hello, or good-bye. But at the second kiss he holds her arm
and pulls her close to him and whispers something in her
ear."

"What?" Lucien says. "What is it he whispers?"

"I don't know. I can't remember," I say.

"Try to think," he says.

"I don't know what he whispers, Lucien."

And before she knows it, he has disappeared through a lovely arch of daylight.

"Au revoir," he says.

Revoir is to see again.

Au revoir is not really good-bye then.

## 18

She submerges herself in water, comes out into sun, then goes back into water again. Il fait trop chaud. Some days the Chinese hat does not seem like much protection.

How we hurried out of our black dresses.

We had a last Spanish dinner together. We played Jacques Brel over and over. We dreamed of Nice and Antibes.

I look out into the blue rectangle pool. I study the perfect stroke of the swimmer.

I let the sun burn me. Children run by. "Regardes! Regardez-moi!" Children push each other into the pool.

She closes her eyes and pictures the young French man she would have done anything for that afternoon next to the fountain, across from the Bar Marseillais. She cries out for the force and beauty of his one life pressing to meet hers.

Over the radio a mournful voice sings, "Don't stop, don't stop the dance." Though radio playing is interdit.

I see a girl giggling with her friends. She can't be more than fourteen. She's wishing that boy would look at her. I look over. He wants me. He's about to ask me, "Qu'est-ce que tu écris?" The young girl is shy. She giggles again. She thinks he is very cute. She is so awkward in her new body, so beautiful in her becoming. No one has taken her to bed yet.

"Regardes! Regardez-moi!"

She thinks of the young French man from the unmade film by the dead Truffaut.

In the notebook it says: "She remembers the dazzling silence they tried to speak through. The perfect forever of his face. She wanted to die."

The boy that the girl is giggling for is reading Breton. He's smoking a cigarette though it too is interdit. He's got that nose. That same long brown hair.

He's reading Breton. This is France, they read la poésie by the piscine.

He asks me for a pen finally. "Qu'est-ce que tu écris?"

"J'écris un roman. Un roman d'amour."

"Tu es anglaise?"

"Non." They can't tell an American accent from an English one and why should they?

He tells me his English is not good.

"Oui."

"I like your cheveux longs," I say. "It reminds me of someone I love. No. Someone I would like to love." It's impossible to say it in French at this moment. I haven't seen Lucien in days.

"Tu connais *Nadja* de Breton?" I ask.

"Non."

He gives me his phone number. He has a phone. He hopes I will call him. He disappears into the changing room.

The French love the surrealists, and why not?

The French are very keen on the breaststroke. And on diving. The children dive again and again into the pool. The parents are giving their instructions. Next to me a young man is reading the palm of a girl in a polka-dotted bathing suit. The news is good. She will be rich, happy, lucky in love. He squeezes her hand. She takes off her bathing suit top. She turns toward me. I glimpse her small breasts. She is lost in the future and in the man who touches her soft hand. Is it you I will love? she wonders, looking at him.

If Lola were here, I would tell her the story of their future. What will happen after only a few years.

She wears a medal of the Virgin between her breasts. She feels me looking at her and for one moment she pulls herself out of the future. She smiles.

I am writing a roman d'amour, I tell her when she asks.

I look into the amorphous water shaped by the tile rectangle pool.

There's no use assigning blame—that much we can agree upon. That much seems right. It's over, that's all; I will never really understand why.

I realize that I am living in the last moments before I become resigned to everything forever. I think to myself that I'd like to touch my father on the shoulder again, offer some small consolation, give my mother a kiss once more.

In the white room, she remembers, they practiced tenir and revenir.

She remembers their arms, like wings.

I am writing a love story far from home.

"Je vais, I go now," I say.

"Bonne chance," I whisper to the girl.


# 19

She feels beauty and then the absence of beauty. She feels the absence of all things. She does not cry. She just stands there and feels herself being stripped of everything. She feels all things being taken away.

She watches three people in the park put up their collapsible table and take out their petitions and pamphlets. She thinks of her older brother once more though it doesn't seem like it should be possible. It seems as if that part of the brain should have somehow shut down. But the circuit mends and the extraordinary brain resumes its sad connection. Even in France, far from home. A woman and two men, reformed drug addicts in the park with their petitions. SIDA. AIDS. A different sort of desperation fills them now.

"Beaucoup mes amis," but I don't know how to finish the

sentence today. "Oui?" "Are dead." They nod.

"Brigitte Bardot a dit: Les chats n'ont pas le SIDA," I say. It's been in all the papers. They laugh. Then one shakes his head. "C'est grave."

"Oui," I say. "Mon frère."

She feels the danger in all things.

She tries to call up the rose light. The Chapelle du Rosaire. She remembers her older brother listening to *Madame Butterfly* on his Sony Walkman. Their father magnifying the columns of names.

She thinks of the hospital room. Lola telling him lies. She thinks of Lola. Her fear of solitude, her fear of death. Her love of convention. She thinks of the word *deception*. The word *defection*. The terrible blind eye.

Sylvia has had a small stroke in the night.

She is sitting with a blanket on her lap next to the bleeding geraniums on the terrace.

"Catherine, Catherine," she cries, "it's been pandemonium around here! Everybody running in and out, bringing cakes," she says breathlessly. "And in the middle of it all the plombier arrives to fix the sink! The one with the cremation society sticker on his car! The ghastly man!"

She tells me of the time he informed the town of Vence that there was water running under the cemetery. "Imagine! Water there was no way to stop! And a meeting was called with the maire. And all the people kept saying over and over, 'The plombier has said the cemetery is filled with water, there is a river underneath the cemetery!' And the maire, *another perfectly awful little man*, stood up and said, 'I will do something I promise. You will not swim in your graves!' "

She tells me of Emil who died and then came back from the dead. "Can you imagine?" she says. "Emil told the story at the town meeting with the maire. At his wake he *saw* his wife wearing a brand-new dress, a shawl, a veil, and when he came back from the dead he asked her, Where is the new dress you looked so mournful in? That dark shawl and veil? And all this he recalled from death! How queer! And later, at the funeral he recounted Camille, at the cistern, in grief putting one leg into the water and then the other, and there were two black dogs there and a white horse and his friend the butcher sitting under the almond tree, afraid, afraid, afraid, all night long, and almonds falling on his head, and Emil remembered all this though he was *perfectly dead*! Just the makings for soup—a hank of hair and bone!"

"Shh—it's OK. Quiet now, Sylvia," I say.

Sylvia trembles and remembers the war. She remembers making false documents in a basement room. "I made them Catholic, but you know those Jews had *terrible* problems, because the Nazis would ask them to say a prayer from the Mass or something *like* that, and of course they didn't know *a thing* about being Catholic, so I began making them Protestants and I told them to go to church in the villages where I sent them. The husbands separated from their wives, and the wives would want to know where I sent their husbands, but of course you see I never *knew* because all those papers were false with made-up names and I never knew what or who or how many. . . ."

Bells continue to ring. "You know the French—many of them would point out the places Jews were living because they wanted their houses. Oh when I think of it! The doctor says I mustn't think of any of it."

I try to calm her down. We talk about the future.

She tells me she would like to go see *The Last Emperor* next week when she's feeling better.

"Well, you know, I don't believe a *thing* that young doctor says. One trusted doctors once."

Her right side is numb.

"I rang up my niece. She's just passed her exam. She may come for a visit. She says she wants to see *the world*! She's young enough to believe she can actually see it! Monica and I once tried, but we got stuck here. It was at a time when we thought that life goes on forever!"

I was well past that time already, I thought.

"You know I made papers for those Jews. Poor things. And

the French, you know, they couldn't be trusted for a minute! They'd point out houses where Jews were staying because they were promised the *real estate!* You are under the impression, my dear, that because you are in France nothing bad can happen to you. But it is an illusion you will pay dearly for." She looks on helplessly. But she even saved *Jews.*

"The French never, never put chrysanthemums in their houses. Chrysanthemums are for the dead. For the graves on Toussaint.

"Poor Lawrence, he thought he was coming to Vence to get better, but he was coming to die."

I sit with her all afternoon in the villa called Paradis. I love sitting here, I tell her, because you can see the sea.

"Yes, but you can't see it today."

"I can see it," I tell her, "even on days it's hazy, because I know it's there."

"Clever you!" she says.

I've brought her a present.

"Don't say it's a cake!" she says.

"No." I need her to see. To write her love poems. To tell her stories. I need her to believe. I open my bag. I've brought her a notebook of her own.

## 20

After college we move to New York and we are filled with hope; anything seems possible. Bleecker Street. A small apartment near the Bowery. We live near the cinema. Near CBGB. She is going to film school. I have found work as a waitress. I want to be a writer.

On the first day of my job there is a power failure, city-wide. It is summer and all the merchants give away their food as it defrosts and melts. We walk around the new city eating free ice creams. At night we wander in darkness down to the World Trade Towers. This is the summer of Son of Sam, the serial killer of women. He *could be anywhere*, we whisper through the black.

She dreams of becoming a director and likes film school. Of course she has doubts, but there are always doubts. On my days off I try to write but I am too distracted; I am too tired. I have not really learned how to work yet, and by the time I have finally begun to concentrate, it is time to go back to the restaurant. I am belligerent with the customers. I am forgetful. I am not a good waitress. In the years to come I will be fired or quit many times from many jobs.

She'll try to protect me from the Middle Eastern men when I take a job at The Magic Carpet. She'll help me check the cash register at 1:00 A.M. when all I can do is curse under the red light, hating everything, their faces, their dogs, their incessant, tuneless music.

For a while I am an artists' model, but it alternately enrages and exhausts me. I became tired of gazing into these men's eyes. Angry at watching them make things out of me. I want to write. I begin to take a series of lovers, something that we somehow think we can bear. First there is the actor in her film project, a handsome, foolish man. Then there is the neighbor down the hall. Then the performance artist. And it goes on and on.

We work on her thesis film together. I write the script and she directs. We are up at six each morning and exhausted at 2:00 A.M. when we fall into sleep, and for several months we feel as if we are the happiest people on the earth. But it doesn't, can't last. The shooting of the film ends. She never has enough money to finish it.

Now and then to console ourselves, we go on a shopping spree with her student loan money or a credit card we can never pay back. We go to Henri Bendel's and buy leather pants. We go to Chinatown. She buys me a jacket, a dress, a Chinese hat.

From time to time my parents come to New York and we have a serious discussion as to what I am doing with my life.

I love them. They are worried about me. I tell them I am going to be a writer, though no one has seen one word. They ask me to be practical. I show no signs of getting married. How will I support myself? *I do not know.* What about children? *I do not know.*

They urge me to go to graduate school, but I know it is the wrong thing to do. I like school too much and can play the game too easily. I know how to please, am too good at manipulation. But instead of saying any of this I simply refuse to go.

My mother reminds me that when I was young I could do anything. The world was mine. I could have everything. I know it is true. I felt that way once.

*I don't recognize my own daughter,* she says. I look at myself in the mirror. I look at my mother. I don't weep. I never weep, not in all those years—not in my whole life—not even when my older brother dies. I don't know why. I think if I started I might never stop.

There is too much rage, too much depression, and I am placed on medication. I vacillate too extremely between despair and joy. I scare Lola. I scare everyone who knows me. When I get a job at Lord & Taylor's, she watches helplessly as I iron my apron in silence. I am fired more and more frequently and so have more time to write. Many nights I cannot sleep and stay up writing.

I am writing prose poems. They seem to be going somewhere; still nothing will give way. I feel I am in possession of some complete freedom that is just out of my reach. I feel faith and then absence of faith. I despair at the limits of things. The limits of language. The limits of love. The limits of my own ability.

She gets a job as a film editor but she rarely gets to edit anything. *This is not how I thought it would be,* she says. She is asked nothing and is paid next to nothing for it. She begins to drink.

I go off my medication without telling anyone. I write so fast sometimes that the words become one straight line. She is afraid and often tries to hide my papers, my pens. But like an alcoholic I've got them hidden all over the house.

I tell her I am Mary the virgin mother of God. I tell her I am a human fountain. I tell her I will be the best writer of my generation. She says you are vain and arrogant to think that. I tell her I am Joan of Arc and I am burning. Everything is on fire.

I become terrified when I get sick, when I have a fever, a bladder infection, the flu, but I rarely go to the doctor. This is one of the hardest things to accept: I have become part of the poor, uninsured.

I try to leave Lola for a man who loves me, who will support me, whose children I will have. A farmhouse in Vermont. My own studio. A simple life. "Maybe there could be a sheep or a goat!" I cry, overexcited. But I can't go. I'm afraid. There are fascists there.

I become more and more reclusive. I will not answer the telephone. I hate surprises. Even the small surprise of who is on the other end of the receiver. This annoys her. We work out a phone code, but sometimes even when I know it is her I will not pick it up.

We go to the movies and afterwards everyone chatters away about the plot, the characters, this scene or that, on and on, but I say nothing. *It's like you're not here at all.*

She wonders why I have no interest in learning how to drive. *I do not know.* This is true of many writers, some writers anyway, but when I tell her this she just shakes her head; it's not a world she cares about anymore. *In the real world*, she says, that's all she cares about, *people do things, people drive cars, people answer phones.* People should be able to do things. It's that simple. Later she'll want to get me a computer and I'll balk again and she will not be able to hide her disappointment in me.

She begins to think she wants something else. She is tired of struggling in film. She is tired of our unhappiness. She decides to go to graduate school in business. This is perhaps the gravest mistake she makes. But she is tired of everything.

Tired of our life. I retire and live off her business school loans with her. She wants me, she says, only to write.

We live in deference to the so-called talent as if it were something that might break or go away.

I stay in bed for days. The days turn to weeks. I cannot lift even my hand from the bed. *I do not feel at home here*, I say. She explains we are in the same apartment we have always been in, that everything is the same. *I am so alone*. Other times it becomes clear that if I do not move I shall die. If I do not go somewhere I will go crazy, and she helps me to move to that place—it might be the coast of Massachusetts or New York State or Maine. But I hardly ever stay. And she comes to get me. *I do not feel at home*.

But it is not always so hard. Sometimes what I feel is quite harmless. The house is filled with gray cats, I tell her one night before we make love. Another day I tell her there is a shining bowl of eggs under the bed. She is interested for a while, curious; but she grows weary even of this. After a while she doesn't want to see cats or mermaids or eggs. She becomes numb. It no longer delights or terrifies. *I am a human fountain*, I cry. *Water spurts from my wrists. My body is covered with eyes*. But she just shrugs. I tell her I am haunted by a woman who cannot stop crying.

In December of 1980, after John Lennon is murdered we think that this is as bad as it gets. We think we know something. But we don't know anything.

Five hundred pages of what I believe to be a novel have accumulated. I carry them around in a shopping bag. She urges me to get it typed. She finds a typist.

Eventually my novel is accepted for publication and she is ecstatic. *This is what we have been working toward all along*.

But I am morose. Happy only for moments. And she is baffled and disappointed by my panic and sadness. For the book jacket I choose a photo that seems to me a total disguise. I want to hide. When the book appears in the bookstores I want to buy them all back. I am appalled when people recognize me on the street from my photograph, because *I do not look like that.*

She mistakenly thinks my life has gotten easier. It is filled with interviews, readings, lectures. But in fact it is just the opposite: life is becoming more and more unbearable, more impossible to live.

After the book is out for a year and has gone into paperback, we must finally face the fact that I will never make any real money; that I am just not that kind of writer.

We go on vacation to Block Island for one week in August. One perfect week. We ride our bicycles fast. In a silly mood we name them Blueberry and Cherry Black. They were horses and we flew on them over hills, past ponds, through water lilies, and we were home: two white rockers on an enormous porch—and the ocean, remember, everywhere.

Life seems good. In the flickering late light of summer on Block Island we pick the names for the children we now want to have. We are serious about this. For a girl: Lily. For a boy: August.

I am dangerously happy.

Back in the dark city I take another lover. And then another. I don't know what I could have been thinking. What I wanted.

She continues to try to please me. I continue to write. But not one word I put down seems to be the right one, seems good enough. She gets a job an hour out of the city. When she gets a car, we go on long weekend drives but we can never drive far enough. She tries to have an affair from time to time, but I have the ability to make anyone she has even the slightest interest in seem ludicrous in a matter of minutes. It's not like it was hard. I remember the "artist" who sold greeting cards, the UPS person. Come on.

She thinks I am too critical of everyone and everything and she is right. I am more and more difficult to be around. I am most critical of myself. I am slowly making it impossible to live my life. Always raising the stakes. For a thrill. I want to keep feeling something. I want to go somewhere new. I am working on a second book.

And then my older brother, who has heard this whole story a hundred times, gets sick and has to go to the hospital. And then we learn he is going to die. But we don't believe it. A new virus. I watch him day after day in the white room. We reminisce: we played in tall grass, we caught imaginary fish. He worked in a huge office in the World Trade Center, the Twin Towers. She becomes afraid for me. No one knows much yet about this terrible disease. She is afraid I will get it too. Or go crazy from loving my older brother whose disappearance, we learn, is imminent.

I destroy my second book. I destroy what suddenly seem false friendships. I eliminate all my lovers. I eliminate almost everything, but still there is no peace, no silence.

Many months later I try to write about the life and death of my older brother. But each sentence seems to erase itself as I put it down. Always now fewer and fewer real words. Already I see where this is leading. Still, I persevere. I finish the book. And the book changes me. It is the hardest thing I will ever do. But it doesn't even come close.

What had made it possible to continue was the ability to make up a life. I was "creative" or "crazy" or "out of control" or whatever—stupid things, but things nonetheless to be. And when I could no longer do it, she did it for me: "writer," "lover," "sister." And I believed her.

*Sister*. And I believed her, even after his death. *Writer*. Even after the book was destroyed.

And when the world suddenly and without warning becomes enormous, a million times its normal size and she is far away and remote, as small as a midget, whispering Catherine, here, over here, and I scream to her "Why is everything so small?" she says, "I am the same size as always," and "you are *not crazy*. I am the same old Lola. And we are home."

But I know what it means when the midgets come.

I begin to try to name ways out of this. Picture ways of escape. The name of the place is France, I decide. I win a big prize. I beg her to leave her job and come with me. We might

start again there. I love her. I want us to be OK, to be together. Forever. I am sure now. I want to live. I want to live
with her in a house in France. Leave this crumbling and
doomed city with all its sadness. And she agrees.

Life without her does not seem like real life.

I believed in stories once and wrote them down. I thought
the work I was doing was more important than it actually
was. That's only natural.

I realize this doesn't even begin to explain our life together. No use explaining. You think we really wouldn't have
needed so much.

We thought we might collaborate on another film together
one day. We thought we might live together in a house in
France.

But I have not forgotten, Lola, the fish or the road or the
red sign we bled by. I have not forgotten your kindness or
the way you helped me get out of bed. Or how so often the
dark world seemed radiant in your presence. Or the hat . . .

And how life does not seem like real life without you. And
that I am sorry. Too late.

## 21

I go to the galerie with another French man, the one who was
reading Breton by the pool, a happy, simple creature.

I realize how much I've needed to see him by the fountain
again. I walk right up to him, "I miss you, Lucien," I say.

He nods, feeling the strange and insistent eroticism of
these days. He eyes the other man suspiciously.

A few days later she sits outside the Bar International and
has a pastis. It is a small gesture, but it is enough. He wanted
to be alone. Now he wants to be with her. He is exerting the
small power he still has. He kisses her twice on the cheeks.
Not a word is exchanged. Not a single apology or explanation.

He opens the notebook. It's been a week. He can't be sure he's the hero anymore.

He sees that she has conjugated the verb *aller* on a page. To go. Je vais, tu vas, il va, nous allons, vous allez, ils vont.

He imagines she'll leave soon. But he doesn't know anything about her—how she loves, or what she wants.

She loves like this: in the neat turn of his head. In cheveux longs. In one or two images. A smile. A few words—"tu viens?" That's all. And they go.

She loves him best, she thinks, when he is in bed next to her, not standing, not selling anything. "You have beautiful hair," she says.

"Non."

As much as I try to darken him, nothing makes him less luminous, nothing makes him seem cloudier, I realize. He rises shining. She takes his penis in her mouth.

Especially because of the week between them, when she sees him naked next to her, she gasps. She can't help but say it sometimes—after lovemaking, after any movement away and then back. She can't help it, the words come—*you are so beautiful!* He smiles. Tonight it is a forgivable sin.

She thinks to herself, you are so beautiful, like a woman. So resigned.

She thinks how they hurried out of their black dresses. Someone in the room puts on *Madame Butterfly*.

She thinks of disappearances.

"You have beautiful hair," she says.

"Non."

She watches the young man who disappeared now disappear into her. He rises above her and watches too.

"We are smoke," she says. And for one moment they are free.

He smiles. Presses his forehead against hers. Closes his eyes.

They lie far apart on the large bed. Related, somehow, but not touching. Together, she thinks, they live the lives of objects in a lonely, surrealist poem: pear and hoof, glove and fig, tambourine and beast.

## 22

He looks at me. We are turning a strange corner.

"Where is your cahier?"

"A la maison."

"Je ne le crois pas," he says. "Tell me a story."

"There was once a young man in France who looked as if he had stepped out of a film by Truffaut. He worked near a fountain and all day he'd dip his hands into the water, into the liquid light. All day long the elegant young man lets water run into his mouth.

"Pretty girls pass all afternoon. They dip their long, smooth arms into the fountain like swans. So many white swans—qu'est-ce que c'est le mot for 'swan'?" I draw a picture for him on a napkin.

"Les cygnes."

"Oui, les cygnes."

He has never seen swans at the fountain he stands at every day, until now.

Once, in her notebook he read, "Le monde du papier." It made an impression on him. He says it a few times now.

"A woman comes and sits at the bar. At the tables around the fountain. She orders a pastis. It comes in a tall glass that says 'Pastis 51.' And all the while the young man is watching and revolving his postcard racks that are outside the librairie/galerie where he works. She swears she can almost feel him on her back as he rotates the colorful cards. He comes and sits behind her. He is wearing a Kenzo T-shirt. She is writing in a notebook and he is so close that if he wanted to he could see what she is writing. He makes her a little nervous."

"Pourquoi nerveuse?"

"Ah, I forgot one of the most important parts of the story," I say. "He is 'sans doute' the most beautiful man she has ever seen.

"She's got on a shirt with a very low-cut back. It's hot and she can feel him staring at her. He gets up again. Goes back to where he was standing. He lights a cigarette. His straight hair falls in his face and he combs it back with his hand.

"In the window of the galerie a book: *L'Intelligence des fleurs*.

"She orders another drink. She can't keep her eyes off him. He's looking at her too. He's standing inside the galerie now looking out. She's beginning to feel a little drunk. Such bright sun. He's following, she thinks another woman now. She keeps seeing him darting in between the art cards: the Picassos, the Dufys, the Matisse cutouts.

"The patron at the Bar Marseillais has been watching the whole thing.

"The young man, the one who is so beautiful, is leaning back now, his fingertips in the water, as if he's part of the fountain. He is beautiful like a woman, n'est-ce pas? she thinks. He is too beautiful for almost everything. I don't know how he walks down the streets safely."

He laughs a little.

"Viens." Come here, she thinks.

"The sound of rushing water floods her. She looks up. He walks over.

"She loved that dangerous afternoon she tried so hard to speak through.

"'Vous parlez français?' he asks.

"'Non. Oui. Non. Un peu,' she says."

"What happens next?" Lucien asks.

"They talk."

"And then?"

"That's all?"

"That's all."

"Oui. That's the end of the story."

"Non. I think he takes her to bed next," he says smiling.

"Vraiment? Tu penses?"

"Oui."

"Then it is a happy story."

"Oui. It is a happy story."

## 23

"I'm tired of you crying all the time," he says as he dresses for work. He's not expecting an explanation. He's not expecting anything.

I kiss him twice, and leave.

I pet cats on my way home, although it feels forbidden somehow. I miss my cat. I miss Coco.

I pass the villa called Paradis. Sylvia sits outside on the terrace, framed by geraniums. "Sylvia!"

"Oh, it's bliss itself!" she cries. "To see you at this hour!"

She's been given another chance. Everything feels precious. She lifts her cup of tea. Sun shines through the bone china.

"Sit down," she says moving her hand to her throat. "And tell me something."

I tell her about a young poet in a blinding red dress. We talk about Nice. So many blue chairs. We talk about Sylvia Plath.

"Yes, I always *forget* she was an American, and that you Americans like to claim her. Of course it was England she loved. Terrible, terrible that she had to die. And that *awful* Ted Hughes, destroying her work. We all took it rather hard here, you know." She looks at me with her watery and ancient eyes. "Though of course it didn't affect Monica—not in the same way." She sighs.

"I never lived, you know, with the right person, the one who could give me the truth, the one who could make me truly happy. I did love Monica though. Don't get me wrong.

"Oh, I don't mean to be summing up."

She talks about her former lovers. The Great Dane, Millicent, Vivien, now dead. She tells me she always knew how taken she was by any woman by her sudden, strange inability to eat cheese.

She tells me about Evelyn. "We were madly in love with each other," she says. "But never at the same time." She laughs.

She talks about Monica, her elegant, aristocratic lover from the fallen empire of L. Sometimes, still, she refers to Monica in the present tense.

She looks at me coyly. "Oh, if I was thirty years younger...."

"Or, Sylvia, if I was thirty years older," I say to her.

"Oh my, I hadn't thought of *that!*" she says.

My hair shines in the light of midmorning. "If you don't want to attract the boys, you're going to have to cut that pretty hair, my dear."

"Who said I don't want to attract the boys, Sylvia?"

"Oh, don't be ridiculous."

That's when I blurt it out—about the man with the cheveux longs.

"I thought you were one of the girls!"

"I am."

"You're not! A young man from town!" She pouts. "Oh, what a *bore!*"

A bug nears her neck. I brush it off. She's not sure whether to slap my hand or caress it. "Yes, I do not like bugs *at all*—sucking my blood or whatever it is they do."

She shows me a picture of herself as a handsome young woman in a coat and tie.

She's pretending she hasn't heard about the man with the cheveux longs.

We make plans to see *The Last Emperor*.

She recounts lover after lover. "I remember following Evelyn from carriage to carriage thirty years ago.... After making love she would always go into another room to sleep because she said *sleep is so personal!*"

She recalls the sixties in London. "The tall gorgeous one with the short, blonde hair from Denmark. We called her the Great Dane. I remember her on the dance floor one night. She was wearing a white dress with one shoulder exposed. She was just gorgeous and all the girls were *fighting* for her. It doesn't seem possible that even the Great Dane is dead!

"Such a shame," she says. "If only I was thirty years younger."

## 24

Finally she tells him about the woman in New York.

"You are a lesbian then?"

"Oui."

He doesn't believe anything. He laughs. Now he's heard it all.

"I don't believe you."

She shrugs.

"Then why me? Pourquoi moi?" He points to his name in her notebook. He points to the bruises he has left on her upper arm simply by holding her.

He lights a cigarette. "Perhaps it is best not to be too happy," he says. "You with your lost lover from L'Amérique and the French man you like to call beautiful.

"You use me," he says. "I see how you stare. You use my profile, my walk. I read while you slept about 'the particular beauty of the French.' I read about the nose, the long hair, everything. I recognized myself there."

"So?"

"Why did you write: 'He is waiting for his life to begin'?"

She knows he's thinking of leaving again. He kisses her. He's becoming afraid of the desire that obliterates all. He's afraid of loving her, this American who goes away. He hates that part of the truth. She knows because it was what he was saying fast and in French while he slept.

He is trying to lose her. She too is trying to lose someone. But everyone comes back. They hear voices. The woman from New York. The family he refuses to talk about. Sometimes they cover their ears. Put pillows over their heads.

He remembers her asking now about les femmes françaises.

"Tell me a secret," she says. But he won't.

They become larger than their small touches, half secrets, retreats. Even he feels it. But still he says, "It's nothing. This means nothing. Rien du tout. Nothing at all."

He remembers now when she asked the name of the waitress. He begins to laugh.

"Why are you laughing."

"It's nervous laughter."

I look at him. I am struck by this confession. This secret. It feels like the only truthful thing he has ever said.

"I want to go to bed with you, but I'm not sure anymore if that's what you want," he says. He is so alone. I can't help thinking it. He writes "Fin" in my notebook. He writes "The End."

"Stop writing that," I say.

He laughs. "Tell me more about the woman from New York. Elle est jolie?"

"Oui, très jolie."

He goes to my photos. "Where is her picture?"

"I don't have one."

"Mais pourquoi? There are many women here." He looks at a few and then hands them back to me.

"Qu'est qu'il-y-a?"

"I can't look at these," he says.

"Pourquoi?"

"Parce que."

"They are lovely, n'est-ce pas?"

"Oui."

I hold them like cards. Like the rare collection they are.

"Never take my photo. Jamais."

"Oui, je sais."

So while he is asleep she gets out her camera. It's black and boxy and she fumbles with it. She can't believe his face. She can't get over the perfect body under the thin white sheets. Through the lens he looks so vulnerable it scares her. She puts down the camera. For a minute she feels like she truly understands him.

"I asked you to put away the pictures of the women," he says the next morning.

"Why do they disturb you?"

"Because they are proof of something I believed did not exist."

I laugh, having caught him believing something.

"Don't be silly, Lucien. Let me tell you about them. I can tell you who the smartest was, the most sensitive, the kindest."

"I can't bear it when you talk that way."

"Mais pourquoi?"

There is no photo of the one she loves most though. That she could not bear. When there should be the person in front of her, there is only the photo. And so no photo.

Like him she does not really believe in photographs.

She tries to imagine Lola but it's getting harder and harder. "Elle n'est pas là," she says out loud.

"Quoi?"

"She is not there."

He shakes his head. "You use everyone," he says.

## 25

I am sitting in light with my American friends in Saint-Paul. Lucien's gone away again.

They have seen Yves Montand. They are Americans; celebrities improve the way they feel.

They have heard from Lola. "She is wondering why you will not return her calls or write anymore."

"It's over now."

"No!" the American friends say. "She's stopped seeing that woman. That affair is history!" they say.

Why are they talking so loud? Nothing they say makes much sense anymore. She thinks they walk through France unscathed, and she is fascinated by it.

"We made an aquatic sighting the other day," my friends say.

"Who did you see?" I ask wearily.

"Guess."

"Brigitte Bardot."

"No. We saw Lucien. At the pool."

"Really?"

"He was wearing a blue bathing suit."

"Let me tell you the rest of it," I say. "He is alone, of course. Even among screaming children and talking teenagers you can pick him out because of the empty space he walks through, the circle he maintains of solitude. He stands at the edge of the pool with his arms folded, brooding. Slowly he bends down and slips himself into the water with utter grace. He does a perfect breaststroke. His head above water. His hair. I see him clearly—that magnificent head. He swims to the other side of the pool, and then slowly and with one sensual movement lowers his head back and his long hair becomes perfectly combed by water, away from his face—his exquisite face."

They sit spellbound. "That's it. That's exactly it!" they say. "You must be in love with him."

I smile. They don't understand that this image of him in water is all I really want. The ability to conjure him.

My American friends say that he is very handsome. They say that they can tell he is moody. They say he is probably a communist. They ask me a lot of questions I don't know the answers to. "Where is he from? What is his family like? What does he want to do?"

But he's unknowable and I don't feel like making him up.

He's exempt from answering such questions, I tell them. Suddenly I feel protective of him, protective of his enormous solitude. He's unknowable, we will never understand him. It feels like he's in some kind of danger. He is gravely misunderstood. I become angry. I'm not about to make him into a character for them. A hero. I can't transform him. He won't let me.

They change the subject. They have looked all morning for the awful stuff Americans call cottage cheese and they can't find it.

"I'm glad," I say. "Cottage cheese in France!"

They find me contrary. A little arrogant, like Lola says, but

I find something a little dense about them; I can't help it. There's something in them that fails to vibrate. But maybe I have been unfair. Maybe I should not have placed them in such exquisite light, where only Lucien can live now.

26

She fits her mouth, which is hotter than the air, tightly around him, a second skin in this torturous heat.

"Un, deux, trois," he counts the deep waves in her hair. "Like a Hollywood film star, une vedette." He smiles.

"Tell me about the book you will write." He moves his mouth now to her breasts.

"I would like to write you a book in which one side of the page is in English, and the other side of the page is the French translation, and every time the book is closed the two sides would kiss. That is the kind of book I would like to write for you."

He smiles. "J'ai envie de toi," he says.

"I love you, Lucien."

"Non," he says. "It is not the truth."

"Si. C'est vrai." She does.

Later he asks her to tell him again what it felt like to open the shutters on a balcony in France for the first time.

"Comme un oiseau," she says, opening her arms. "Like a bird."

He smiles.

I picture how he will look in the morning at the fountain. The pattern of the plane trees on his back. I picture him walking through the Place du Peyra. I feel him enter the place in my heart, in my imagination, that has always existed for him. Waited for him. This beautiful, detached, incomprehensible aspect of myself.

I feel the specificity of love. It is this one man in one place at the end of a century. A man smiling after a woman says she feels like a bird.

"I love you."

"Non."

"Yes."

He shrugs.

He takes her from behind. She gasps. "You have beautiful hands," she says.

"Non."

"What is the word for 'hands'?"

He can't speak. He moans. Maybe hours pass.

He turns her over and over. Again, again.

He lies on her back. "Am I too heavy?" he asks.

"Non. Tu es parfait."

"Tell me a story," he says.

"I slept with a girl with crimson hair once." She tells him about a simple walk in the rain to get stamps and how somehow she ended up again, despite intentions, in the rain, in the afternoon, in a strange woman's bed. But that was long ago.

"You have beautiful hair."

"Non."

"You have beautiful ears."

His hair is longer than hers.

"I forgot to tell you that we made love that afternoon in the dressing room of the Galeries Lafayette. We were buying things, lipsticks, perfumes and then we decided to try on lingerie, because after all this is France. We could see the petites feet of the saleswoman going back and forth the whole time. French music was playing. After that we were starving. We ate a big meal. Pasta. Truite. Cèpes. We drank vin rosé."

She closes her eyes. "Grappa."

She thinks of her many crimes. The girl with the crimson hair a minor one in the scheme of things.

She tells him about the Chinese man she saw in the film, his hands turning the water red. She tells him about the little emperor demanding, "Ouvrez la porte." She laughs.

She tells him about the rose light in the Chapelle du Rosaire, Matisse's Chapel.

He says it: "You are beautiful." Something about him saying it stings her.

She has been accused of using her beauty recklessly. She has been accused of possessing a genius that makes life unbearable. Of all the things that seems the most unfair. What genius?

She is the first to admit that at times she has been unusually cruel. She's not sure why anyone has stood for it. She thinks she would be different given a second chance. But she's stopped believing in second chances. Or even in first chances. She is becoming more and more like the beautiful young man.

She tries to picture the woman lying on her bed in college. Her arms pinned behind her head like wings.

She licks the inside of his ear.

One wants to begin to trust again—even the trompe l'œil.

There should have been more room for tenderness.

He opens his arms: "Comme un oiseau," he says. He's falling asleep.

She closes her eyes and is surprised to see Matisse sitting on his balcon in Nice, looking at a woman, a bird, a hat, some fish in a bowl, turning them over and over in search of serenity, until he sees a pattern finally, turning them over until they glow.

## 27

My American friends and I go to Villefranche to see the Cocteau Chapel. When we get back, I walk into town and he is standing in the night next to the black water of the fountain waiting for her.

"What are you doing here?" she asks. He gives her a brutal, unforgiving look.

I fear for them. They will play this out for me. I use everyone, he has said it too.

"What are you doing here?"

"Waiting," he whispers.

"For what?"

"Where have you been?" he demands.

"Villefranche."

"Oui? Come with me."

"I walked down a covered street called the rue Obscure. I went to the Cocteau Chapel."

"La Chapelle Saint Pierre," he corrects her.

"Oui. La Chapelle Saint Pierre."

She lies on his bed. She reads to him from the guidebook about the chapel: "On the left side of the nave is Saint Peter betrayed. The apostle, handed over to the soldiers of Pilate, is mocked by them. He has denied his master. The cock crows. Saint Peter weeps and remembers that Christ has foretold to him this denial."

Lucien is silent. Like everything, he has a private notion of sin. Feelings she can't begin to comprehend.

He doesn't understand anything about this woman. She prays to the Virgin. She lights candles in the dark cathedral. "Each light was a life," she tells him. She makes love with women. She likes Michael Jackson. She begs him to go to bed with her. She cries for New York. She cries all the time. She writes long letters to her mother. She likes Wittgenstein.

In the night she asks him to teach her some French slang. She writes down branche, digne, prendre la tête, casser les pieds, dégueulasse. They laugh.

She wants to know the difference between the names Stéphane and Etienne. She wants to know about the memory of water. She wants him to explain the new philosophy of Bernard Henri-Lévy, she tells him. She saw him once on television.

She's trying to ask him serious things but she's holding her glowworm green pen from the Prisunic and he laughs. "Qu'est-ce que tu as dit?" he smiles.

She realizes that her "genius" is hidden from him by the barrier of language. She sounds like an idiot, she realizes that, or a grown child. He looks at her strangely in the dark holding the pen.

He can't stop seeing swans now at the fountain. Swans, where there were no swans.

She has an innate American idealism he has no part in. There were books she wanted to write. There was an older brother. They ran in the tall grass in the American summer. "More than anything," she says, "we just wanted to live then."

Lucien looks at me curiously.

"Later there was the glass eye. The fever. The malady of the brain."

He doesn't trust anything. He sits up. Goes to the window. "Come back," she says. She walks toward him. She can almost touch him. But then he pulls back. "Non." He walks around the perimeter of the room, goes to the window and leans out. He feels caged. He feels confined by this sad narrative. "Come back." She tries to touch him. Maybe she could comfort him. "Non."

He lies back on the bed, incapable of being consoled.

"I don't want this anymore," he says. "J'ai honte."

"You don't mean a thing you say."

He turns from her. "I've got to leave. I can't stay here." He gets up. He moves toward the door.

"Why?"

He pulls his hair back tightly from his face. "It is not possible to explain to you," he says sarcastically. "I don't want you."

"Why?"

"You are ugly from so much crying."

She covers her face with her Chinese hat. "Oui, c'est vrai."

"Je m'amuse," he says. "Je suis seul. I am alone."

"La Coste," she says, "une chemise française." She outlines

the little alligator.

"I can't help you with what you want."

"I don't know what I want, Lucien."

"You know."

He takes my hand and squeezes it tightly.

"No. Do not touch me. Je suis dégueulasse."

"Oui," he says, releasing her hand. Laughing. "Good-bye," he says in English. His perfect profile.

"J'ai honte," he says. "Et toi, tu es folle."

"Bye-bye, Catherine," he says, in English.

It is the first time he has said her name. "Good-bye, Lucien."

He comes over to where she is lying.

In the room they practice honte and au revoir. Rien and fin.

He begins to undress her. "No one can help you." He gets up. He scrutinizes her body from some distance. "Viens ici," she says.

"Non."

He walks back and forth.

She puts on her robe.

"Non," he says and opens it. She moves away. He begins to touch himself. He stares at her. He closes his eyes. Her nipples are a rose pink. "The flower of America," he says.

They're both crying.

"I don't want this anymore."

"Va," I say. "Allez. Go, then." One swings between romantic impossible hope and no hope at all. Every degree of abandon, refusal, detachment. My own struggles played out in them.

"There is no talking," he says.

"Take off your clothes," she begs.

I write: In the agony of the afternoon, she licks the perfect rim of his penis. He presses her head hard, harder to him. He pulls her cheveux longs. She opens. The exotic flower of the woman.

He turns her over gently. Gently Lucien or she will break. She kisses him everywhere. Her dazzling mouth. A blinding scarlet covers his body. She leaves her mark.

"I am the fountain you drink from," I whisper to them. "I am the water you cannot live without. Remember how hot it gets." They shudder with recognition and desire.

"Help us," they beg.

He closes his eyes. He tries to remember a time before her, but he can't. "J'ai soif," he says moving his tongue deep inside her. For hours he stays there with her. Incapable of moving. Of going anywhere.

When he lifts his head finally he sees that her toes are pointed. He laughs. It's hopeless. He kisses her feet and weeps.

She tells him a story. Her mother taking her to ballet class five times a week. Her toes bleeding. Red feet. Red shoes. It's not meant to be an excuse. She holds two red feet in her hands and weeps.

He moves next to her. "Tell me the story again," he says.

She takes his arm. What can account for this delicacy, this sweetness I feel suddenly? I smile. For one prolonged moment I feel something like peace. She kisses him on the forehead. He holds her breasts, like two white birds. He shocks me—his innocence, his tendresse.

I know everything that will happen now.

## 28

A woman, x, and a man, y, plan to meet at the prearranged coordinate, z, a fountain on the Place Antony Mars in the south of France, on some late afternoon in summer at the end of the twentieth century.

Both walk slowly, inevitably to z, embracing their common fate and now as they stop and turn, each other. Y, a man with cheveux longs, clearly French, kisses x twice on the cheeks. It is as if he has stepped out of some unmade film of the dead Truffaut. She looks to be German or Scandinavian, possibly English or American, and is wearing a Chinese hat. The sun is very bright, so bright in fact that sometimes one or the other, and sometimes both, seem to disappear in it. He circles her slowly. She sits stationary at a white plastic table, the kind that have become "la mode" in France in the last few years. He circles the fountain, the periphery of z, slowly, looking at her with some exasperation.

"Il fait chaud," he says.

"Non, il fait beau."

"Il fait chaud."

"Such bright, white light."

"Oui, la lumière. Speak French."

"Oui, la lumière."

She conjugates vouloir. Vouloir is to want.

She watches him appear and disappear, appear, disappear.

"This reminds me of another savage and beautiful afternoon."

"Encore?"

"In the savage and beautiful afternoon we tried to speak. You said: 'Where do you live?' I said: 'New York.' It was a time when I was still hoping you might save me."

"Oui," he says, "comme Prince Charmant, sur le cheval blanc." He laughs.

She claps her hands. "Are you ready? Vous êtes prêt? Are you ready now?"

She stands up. "La première position," she says, and arranges his arms and legs into the first position of ballet. He's so beautiful.

"La deuxième."

He holds the position for a moment and then breaks it.

"You thought I could save you," he says. "You wrote it in that notebook."

"La troisième. Parfait!" He holds the pose.

"Already, you knew there was nothing I could do for you." He moves away.

"I asked: 'Where do you live?' You said: 'Near the cemetery.' I asked: 'Where were you born?' You said: 'The most beautiful coast in the world.'"

"No one understands why you have come to my country,"
he says. "L'étrangère, they all say."

She cries. "But I remember the beautiful forever of the
perfect afternoon. The beauty by the fountain. And cheveux
longs."

The shimmering surface of the afternoon. A man carrying
two iced figures nears the plastic table. "La femme qui
pleure," he says. "Chante avec moi." He begins in English the
song she has taught him.

> "Row, row, row your boat.
> Gently down the stream,
> Merrily, merrily, merrily, merrily
> Life is but a dream."

"You were already trembling then," she says.

"Yes, in anticipation."

"Crying."

"Yes, for joy. In grief."

"'J'ai peur,' you said."

"Yes. Already that first day there was une chambre
blanche, chauve-souris. . . . A black and white film. An angel."

"You were expecting maybe a miracle." He smiles.

There is a close-up of the young French man. A profile.
And then the slow-motion turn of his head. A panoramic
gaze.

"You are an angel," she says.

He laughs. Takes her Chinese hat.

She takes it back.

"She remembers the dazzling, the catastrophic afternoon."

He tries to remember that first day. "Already," he says,
"you knew you were doomed."

"Stop," she says, running her finger down his arm, his
chest. The beautiful surface of skin.

"La dernière position," she says.

"Non" he says, "pas encore."

"Oui," she says.

He offers his hand, and she steps into the gesture.

"I love you," she says, entering the illusion like almost everyone. "I love you." Each word a boat.

He shakes his head. "It is only a dream," he says. "A lie. I thought you were different."

He takes her hand and holds it under the rushing, brilliant stream of water and then releases it, and they stand like that.

She in her Chinese hat.

He with his cheveux longs.

Not touching, not saying one word.

Unaccountably there is a dizzying movement of the camera and they are seen suddenly from high above. The camera hovers. Something else hovers. It is, we see, one of the beautiful angels of France. The angel weeps. It begins to rain.


## 29


"I thought you said it never rained in summer."

He laughs.

It is night now. They turn and walk toward the cemetery. He guides her up the steep stairway placing the palm of his left hand on her back. He moves the other arm around her waist and presses the palm of the right hand against her heart. He applies the smallest pressure to her chest and whispers "Arrête."

"Stop," he says, in a heavily accented French.

"Ouvrez la porte," she says, giggling. The man opens the door.

In the room there is a bed, a lamp, a book next to the bed. A strange white light shines through the window. Light the cemetery gives. It reminds her slightly of night in the great illuminated city. "Home," she says, but that of course is not it.

She thinks of her city—silent now, very dark. Inconceiv-

Her dazzling body falls forward onto him. She covers him with a veil of hair and tears. She is afraid. She wants something that doesn't change. Something permanent.

She'll never go far enough.

He turns her over with an eerie precision and takes one foot and then the other and places them on his shoulders. He holds her ankles and steers her so that her head is touching the floor. Off the edge of the bed, beheaded as she is, only a torso now, he drives into her with new ferocity.

She tries to speak, but it is useless.

"My God," he says in English, laughing.

She curls into herself on the floor. He looks at her from the bed. Her body divides into two perfect shapes: the back, the buttocks.

She seems to be floating.

I go over to them and pick up hairpins from the floor, the drenched bed. I examine the black book.

"Look," I say to him. "She is dreaming her way home."

ably tragic. She can't imagine.

"J'ai peur," the woman says to the man, digging her fingers into his upper arm and doing a quick little pirouette so that now she suddenly faces him. There is terror in the eyes of the woman who stands on tiptoe and searches his face for some sort of explanation. "Je ne comprends pas," she says.

"Tu ne comprends rien," the man smiles. She releases him. He directs her to the bed.

"Yes, this I still understand," she says.

I know I am sounding less and less like myself. More like—quoi? a nouveau roman perhaps—a borrowed voice. Still one feels lucky to sound like anything at all. To be able to say anything, to feel anything.

He hovers above her. Her arms encircle him. She feels the metal of his belt buckle against her lips.

"Non." He pulls away, gets down on his knees and watches her, observes her face, the two lines in her forehead that mean she is tired, the slightly open mouth. He holds her ankles in his hands and slowly moves them apart.

"Il fait chaud ce soir," she says and lies back on the bed. Slowly, everything is slowly, he undoes the six straps of her sandals. He pulls the straps tight and then loose. Six times on one foot. Six times on the other foot. He glimpses the golden brown pubic hair beneath her skirt.

She sits up and sweeps the hair to the top of her head and then tilts the head back. He studies her carefully, intently, her forehead, nose, chin, throat. She lets her hair fall and then says again, "Il fait chaud." She asks him to bring—what is the word—her pocketbook. "Where?" She stretches her feline body. "Là," she points and he crawls to it on all fours.

From her bag she takes a small round box of hairpins which she hands to him. She turns so that she is facing the wall. He pulls the hair to the top of her head as he has watched her do and attempts to fasten it there. Long curling tendrils escape his every effort and he sighs. "Do not give up so easily," she says. "Comment?" She unbuttons her blouse and neatly folds it. Then her brassiere. It opens in the front, the back shaped vaguely like a heart. Her breasts, released from the elastic and bone and lace, swell.

She sings the birthday song, softly, off-key. Today is my birthday, she says. Though it is not true.

He sees that the edges of her ears are red and that she has a slight heat rash along the back of her neck. Alternately he feels tender then hostile then indifferent toward her.

She raises her arms to check her hair and he takes this opportunity to place his nose under her arm, breathing deeply. He runs his mouth along the slightly roughened skin of the American, cleanly shaven. He bites her, but gently. She wants him to bite her harder, hurt her somehow—make her feel something. But he won't.

She takes a small mirror from the leather bag and fingers the curls he has fashioned with the hairpins, approving of the job he has done. "Perhaps you are a coiffeur," she says, laughing. He moves his mouth to her rose nipple. She observes him in the mirror, a ravenous and fragile child. When she has had enough she nudges him away with her elbow. He goes around her back over to the other breast and it is the same thing. She watches him and then brushes him away tenderly with one white wing. She turns to face him. She tries to tie his hair in a ponytail. "Non," he says

"Mais il fait chaud." She tries again.

"Non."

Slowly, she unbuttons his shirt, she counts each button, un, deux, trois, quatre, cinq, six, sept. "You are like a child." She outlines the rib cage with her mouth, presses where she imagines the heart to be.

She unfastens the familiar belt now and slips his penis from his pants. It has a life of its own. It is at a particularly lovely angle from his body, she thinks. "L'explorateur," she calls it.

Forcing her down, he pins her hands to the bed. He is more erect now, harder. He straddles her, kneeling, putting his knees under her arms. He raises himself, slowly above her so that he is just out of her reach. Her tongue is barely able to

graze his underside and then not. He sways rocking bac forth, back and forth. She struggles to get free. She tries raise herself on an elbow. "Non." He watches her. She struggles to meet him. She is wet. "Let me go," she says

"Non."

"I want you."

"Non."

"Please."

"Speak French." And with that he releases her hands, back and thrusts himself into her mouth. There's a funn dipping motion. It's getting hard to describe this anymo It's getting more and more difficult. He takes himself ou her mouth and with one hand pulls her skirt up around waist and begins to touch her gently. He smiles and shal his head at her wetness. His long hair hangs over her. "T comme un petit cheval," she says.

She bends her knees, throwing him off balance and he topples in mock defeat. "Do not give up," she says, "so e ily." Parting her legs, muttering in French, he enters her she is laughing and asking, What are you saying? He cov her mouth with his hand.

He moves his hand to her throat as he thrusts harder harder. "You're choking me," she says. "You're choking Then nothing. And I would like to help her, but I can't.

The black book falls to the floor, and she looks up terr "Non. It has no meaning," he says in English.

He sits up and he is deep inside her and he is now sw ing and sweating, and asking for something. She doesn't know what. She tells him, she keeps telling him what she wants. What she needs. She wants to be on top now.

"Speak French."

She finds a way to say it.

"Bon."

He watches as slowly the strands of her hair escape the pins with the violence of her motions. She takes his small surrender and rides—somewhere far away, with him. "T comme un petit cheval."

# Part Three

# 1

I imagine him on his moto passing buses on the winding
streets, swerving, just missing an oncoming car. France, my
American friends have told me, has the highest accident rate
in the world. He is reckless in his passivity. He could never
make the choice to die, it's not in his nature, but he might die
anyway because of poor judgment or no judgment at all.

These intimations of doom—I can't help feeling them
today. I order another drink.

He disappears often now. He can't be counted on. He's
there and then he's gone. Days pass. There is no finding him,
not on any street. He's next to the fountain. But she's afraid;
she won't go there.

In the dream they are drinking wine on the terrace of the
stone house in the bright sun. "The air is like a furnace, n'est-
ce pas?" she says to him. They're holding off as long as possible before going inside, but they can't wait any longer now.
One of them is about to lead the other into the darkened
stone room, into the white-sheeted bed for a long afternoon
of lovemaking, when the bee stings, a bee in a glass swal-
lowed down with a last gulp of wine. And the swelling
begins. All is changed in an instant. A perfect afternoon, it
would seem, and then the bee, fever, ice packs, the hista-
mines rushing to assist—they are mortal.

I see him from afar—stooping over to talk to the albino
midget who gesticulates madly. I want to save him from his

future, from the lips of the albino midget that do not stop. I put my hand on his back. He turns. Everything seems symbolic in this light. He's lost in a story of Marseille, of sailors, an illicit cargo, an arrest.

Such thoughts. It's because he vanishes so often, this elusive center. He is important because he reinforces her worldview, all she believes. Everything vanishes, everything disappears. She is grateful to still believe something, even if it is something like that. When she starts believing in nothing, as he does, that is when life becomes truly dangerous. And it is a dangerous life for him, she thinks. Sad in ways he has already incorporated.

Still, I would like to think that maybe he believes in something: le cinéma, for instance, la poésie.

"Lucien," I say. "Ça va?"

We are guests of this earth. It is obvious. Born in silence and forced into speech where we are strangers.

He stands indifferent in the perfect and indifferent afternoon.

"Oui," he smiles. "Ça va."

We walk down the street together. We pass a mime troupe, making gestures in the air. Everything seems portentous. I can't help but see it that way.

"I've missed you," I say.

"Non," he says.

He wants no one, most of all not an américaine, invading his private world, where he sits in the dark watching film after film.

We go to the bar. Order drinks. We look around for something to say. We're uncomfortable. It's only been a few days, but it feels like a long time.

I make up a story about the woman at the next table. "She sits," I tell him, "at this café each night until it closes. She's heartbroken. She orders something to eat. She cries.

"There is the face of the boy she once loved. All over town.

"Look at the tender pear, cut into pieces on the white plate in front of her. Beside it a piece of cheese.

"Someone is driving recklessly in the night. We will never see him again."

2

He draws a map of France on the table at the bar. He's more willing to speak English tonight. He points to the southwest coast.

"Not another geography lesson," I say.

"Non."

He keeps his finger on the spot. "I was born here," he says. "In a small village near Biarritz." He looks at me strangely. He has a sister. He used to work with his father in the market.

He points to another place on the map. He was in an accident when he was seventeen. He likes to fish. His finger moves toward home. "It is the most beautiful coast in the world," he says.

"Yes," I say, "because you were born there."

I tell him we were born next to the same ocean. He finds this preposterous. He laughs out loud.

He lived his first twenty years on the border of Spain and the sea and now he lives at the border of Italy and the sea. He smiles.

Nizza, the Italians say, as if in a dream.

He begins to talk about where he might go on vacation in the fall. He's got the month of October off. "Berlin, peut-être, ou peut-être Hamburg." He draws a map of Germany and asks me to find Hamburg. I'm wrong. He laughs. "You see, I am right about the Americans."

Maybe he'll go to Portugal. Of course he'll spend a little time in the mountains of France.

"In the book it will say that he loved France most." He nods. "Maybe one day you will go to les États-Unis."

Tonight for the first time he says peut-être.

"Californie?" I ask.

"Non," he says.

"Not New York?"

"Si. Peut-être New York. Perhaps New York," he says in English.

He broke his back playing soccer ("French football," he says) and for a year he was in a wheelchair.

He works in the galerie with his sister's husband and his cousin. It is not that interesting for him.

He looks small suddenly, in the dark, at the bar. He falls silent. "What is it, Lucien?"

"Many things are difficult," he says. "Many things are difficult for me."

He tells me he is not as intelligent as I think; it is only because he is French that he knows so many things. "They teach you things in French schools," he says.

He was a good student once, he tells me. He liked science and math. When he was fourteen his parents were divorced and he was left alone. He had too much freedom, he says, or something. He didn't study hard enough. "It is a sad story," he says in English, with his heavy French accent. He didn't pass the bac. I think of the stupidity of a school system that looks so early, that judges so quickly. As a result, I know, he has been denied access to many things. "I am not smart," he says, and he believes it. The worst part is that he believes it.

"This could not happen in America," I tell him. "There are more chances there."

"I am not intelligent. It is only what you need me to be."

"Non. Intelligence cannot be measured by school or success," I tell him. "Intelligence is something else."

"You are wrong."

"No, I am not."

He is waiting for his life to begin. It never will.

He tells me of himself as a little boy. A wild child with "dix chats sauvages." I picture him bending over, his hair falling in his face, trying to touch them, giving them milk.

He can't stop talking tonight. When he was sixteen he worked in the market with his father.

He says he would like to come to New York to buy and sell books.

He practices his English on the way home looking in all the shop windows. "What is the word for 'stylo'? What is the word for 'chaussures'? For 'boîte aux lettres'?"

"Mailbox."

As we undress I think of the boy with too much freedom. "What will it say in the book?"

"In the book it will say he was born on the most beautiful coast in the world. In the book it will say he fed dix chats sauvages. That he was intelligent, and he did not know it. That he was beautiful."

He pets my mane of savage hair tentatively. "What is the word for 'lion'?"

"Lion," I say.

"C'est le même mot."

"Oui." Slowly he opens my legs.

"What is the word for 'sauvage'?" He looks at me hard from above. Amazed this night as if he has never seen my body before. As if this is our first time.

"Thighs," I tell him. "Breasts."

Afterwards he is quiet. Then, "What is the word for 'cendrier'?"

"Ashtray," I tell him.

"Oui, ashtray."

He picks up a magazine next to my bed. Patti Smith is on the cover. "Elle est fantastique!" he says. He knows that once she lived with Sam Shepard. I smile to hear him say Sam Shepard in his accent. As he's drifting off to sleep he tries to remember the film Sam Shepard was in with fire, non, on the plains. . . .

I try to stay awake. I don't want him to go away yet. "Tu dors maintenant," he whispers. The word for "dormir" is sleep. His eyes are closed. He tells me he saw *Star Trek II* on television last night. The word for "télévision" is television.

"Kirk is not a capitaine, but an admiral. Spock is dead. But in *Star Trek III*, il revient." Il revient—he comes back.

He tells me of a planet where everything is named for women. He smiles. Oui. Daphne . . . Véronique . . . Claudine. . . .

The word for "sky" is ciel.
The word for "heaven" is ciel.

3

That night in his room I tell him that one evening once she wore dolphins in her hair.

"We loved the Hôtel Rivoli on the rue Pastorelli in Nice. We lay listening to the waves. She drew me a map of Nice. None of these things are ever forgotten," I tell him as he unzips my dress.

"Meet me here," she said. "Tonight. I'll have dolphins in my hair."

"Go on," he says, unfastening my brassiere.

"I went to the hotel." He puts his head on my thigh. "I asked for room fifty-six." He opens my legs. "I did everything she told me."

He's becoming addicted to her body. She can tell by the way he touches her now. And the stories. So many stories.

Nice, she thinks, is a long way off. She is finding it more and more difficult to leave the town where she knows he is standing, next to the fountain. He is holding her world in place. A moody and beautiful weight at the center of things. She wants to put herself under him like paper. She wants him to hold her down.

Sometimes he makes her laugh and she likes that. He has an odd assortment of English. Probably from the English women he's brought here on occasion. He knows how to say "pull up the sheets." "Turn over on your side."

She laughs.

"Tell me a secret," he says.

"What kind of secret?"

"You know."

"The next morning in the Hôtel Rivoli we drank pample-mousse juice."

He laughs. "Tell me another one."

I tell him I have been with women who love men.

"You mean women who are not lesbians?"

"Oui."

"How many?"

"Beaucoup. I meet them. They are everywhere. I tell them how I will make them feel. And exactly how I will do it."

"And then?"

"And then they resist. But not for long."

"And then?"

"And then I make them feel that way."

"There are many women like that?"

"Oui."

He laughs again. It's nervous laughter.

"Women are so beautiful in their curiosity," I say, "their openness to everything. They are not like men."

He turns away.

It is a mistake to think that because our vocabularies are not large that we cannot hurt each other.

I have gotten my hair cut a little so that now Lucien's and mine are the same length. He pulls my cheveux longs. "I like it when you do that," I say.

"What else do you like?"

"Many things."

"Like what?"

"I like it when you pull my arms back, comme ça, like wings."

"Tell me the names of the women."

"What women?"

"The names of the women you have loved."

I look at him. He is blurry with pleasure.

"Go through the alphabet," he says.

"Oui?"

"Commence avec A."

"OK," I say. "A is for Annalise."

"Annalise," he repeats.

"B—Brett."

"Brett."

"C would have to be Cynthia. She was my first girlfriend. We were in high school."

He smiles. A universe of women.

"D, let's see, D is for Dominique."

"Dominique! Elle est française!"

"Oui."

He's losing track of the letters. I never get to L. I don't have to say her name. He pulls my cheveux longs. My delirious and passionate guest.

He gets up in the middle of the night to open the window. I kiss him as he gets back into bed and we start again, rotating this swollen, beautiful globe all night. A. B. C. D. Slowly we raise the sun into the sky.

4

"What did you do today?" he likes to ask.

"I went to a funeral."

"Mais pourquoi?"

"Parce-que c'est intéressant. It was someone's great-aunt. It was someone's grandmother. She must have been very, very old."

"What makes you say that?"

"Because it was a happy funeral. Nobody cried much."

He laughs.

"Qu'est-ce que tu as fait aujourd'hui?"

"I went to Tourrettes-sur-Loup." I open my notebook and

show him what I've copied down from a plaque on a house there: "Francis Poulenc de 1952 à 1955 sejourna plusieurs étés dans cette maison. Son opéra 'Les Dialogues des Carmelites' est signé Tourettes-sur-Loup, août 55."

He's surprised. He didn't know about this. I am teaching him things about his France.

"What did you do today?" he asks.

I saw a wedding.

"Oui?"

"La mère avec un chapeau noir with a feather comme un oiseau. A short chartreuse jacket and a short black skirt. Glittering jewels in the pattern of a comet near the ankles of her silk stockings. Everyone dressed to perfection, even in this small town, because this is France.

"In all the photos the feather will be in the face of the man on the step above the mère. Rice and pigeons cover the sky. And the white veils of the beautiful bride."

"I was getting my lunch then," he says. "I saw the bride. She was not that beautiful."

"All brides are beautiful, non?"

"Non."

"I followed a man carrying a baguette away from the wedding. . . ."

"I don't want to hear about the men you like."

"Why?"

"I don't."

"Just one," I say. "There's a young man who appears in a doorway with a flourish. He is extremely handsome and strange. I think that he was Franz Liszt in another life." Lucien laughs. "He moves with great grace to the tables holding a newspaper, then crosses his leg, opens the paper, and is absorbed in an article all in one fluid motion, all with astounding grace. He sits next to a fountain. He is alone."

Lucien smiles.

"It is a beauty unseen in this century." Something one might live for.

Lucien covers his face with his hand. Sighs. "Non."

"I am struck by the solitude of this beautiful man when I see all the other young people of this town together in groups, at the bars, at the cafés, everywhere, kissing each other twice, three times on the cheeks."

"Why is he so solitary, the man at the fountain?" Lucien asks.

"No one knows. There is no reason."

"Si," he says. "There are reasons."

"What are they?"

He smiles. "There is a solitary woman too," he says. "Une étrangère. She is toute seule. Ask any man here. She is très sérieuse. She has many secrets. She writes her secrets in a cahier. She's afraid of bats. She has three waves in her hair."

"She sounds like someone I know."

"Ah," he shakes his head, "je ne sais pas."

"How good is her French?"

"Not good."

"I'm sure I know her then."

"Something else: she cries all the time."

"How do you know so much about her?"

"I watch. She drinks a lot. Sometimes the solitary man and the woman sit together at a café. But they are still alone."

"They are a good match then."

"Pas vraiment. They are both too alone. Non, that is not it; they are both too selfish."

"She thinks he is méchant," I say.

"Yes. She is right. She thinks a lot. She is smart."

"She would like to go home with him. She would like him to take her to bed. She doesn't ask for much."

He smiles. "She does," he says. "She asks for a lot. Someone less solitary might not notice what she asks for, but the man knows."

"He is intelligent."

He just stares at her.

They feel the tug of the silence they were born in. They are fighting to stay in this. But it is hard.

She'd like to live.

She thinks of the word *avec*. It is the only word that comes to her and suddenly she is at the limits of language and desire. The solitary woman takes the solitary man's hand. And they go. In French: Ils vont. They go.

<h1 style="text-align:center">5</h1>

We sit at the Bambou. It's a hot summer night.

"No one knows why he drives that Pontiac here," I say. "I know, though. It is because his mother is American."

"Non, he is French. You are making it up."

"He may seem French through and through, but something gives him away. The way he leans, rests one arm on the car door, some small mannerism, some optimism you know nothing about."

"You are completely folle."

I shrug. "There is the one with the dress shop," I say, "in Cagnes-sur-Mer. Or the salon de thé. Her name is Solange."

He makes one of his French expressions.

"Look at that woman," I say. "She's very tired because she's slept all night on the beach in Nice. It's where the junkies sleep too. And each morning at seven the pompiers wake everyone up with their water and they hose the syringes off the rocks."

He looks at me. "C'est vrai? How do you know that?"

"Three thieves told me once. A strange job," I say, "for the pompiers of Nice. Putting out such fire.

"Those women are Arab," I tell him. "They are in love. They work for her father. His name is Faisal."

I tell him about the horse we had named Cherry Black. I tell him of catching fireflies in a jar. Fishing. Catching imaginary fish with my older brother. "To me those fish were real."

He smiles. "Why so many stories tonight?"

"I miss home," I say. "I miss everything."

I feel the ending of all things. "It is some small protection against the overwhelming desire to suffer. As you are, Lucien." I guess I still think he might save me.

The stories had been a means of engagement. The stories had been a home, for a while.

"Say it in French," he says. "Speak French."

Really she is just stalling for time.

"I don't know how to say it. Ce n'est pas grave."

## 6

He wants her to beg for him and she is willing to—because some things sometimes must be begged for. Her pride falls away. Not that she knows much about pride, despite the accusations of anger and arrogance. Despite the accusations of being guilty of possessing beauty and talent and of having used those gifts aggressively—abused those gifts—this woman who now can barely move, who is stones in the street, who is the pale and ruined wall.

He's punishing her because he saw her in town one day with another man. A friend is all. Allan, the Australian. But he's not sure. He won't talk to her.

She goes to the marché and watches everything from a stone bench near the cathedral. But she stays long after there is any more to watch. It's the paralysis. The feeling of the uselessness of doing anything, going anywhere.

He's teaching her how to be only a woman in a white room with a book next to the bed.

She had called out to him: "Attends."

He said, "Non."

He is punishing her for walking away from him the other day. For not moving toward him at the same moment he moved toward her.

There should have been more allowance for hesitation. We should have been less quick to judge.

She goes to the bar. Men circle her. "Vous êtes belle," they say, but she doesn't care, she doesn't believe it. Why does he move away then? She is not beautiful enough. She is incapable of holding his attention. What good is beauty that does not arrest? She thinks of Breton: "Beauty is convulsive, or not at all." So not at all. This is something she guesses she must believe.

He is punishing her for using her resemblance to the most beautiful actress.

She can't find the pattern. There had been one once. There had been a reason for things, but she had lost it. It happened in France. That's all she can remember. But the design had been imposed; it had never been hers. How else to account for its disappearance seemingly overnight?

Other men ask her to eat with them, to dance, to look for champignons, but she wants him—the one who offers nothing.

He appears out of nowhere.

She tells him a story about the sirocco. "The sirocco comes driving the Sahara desert onto the Renaults, onto the Peugeots, into our throats. We can't move. We can't even lift a hand to brush the sand from our foreheads. It's the end of gesture. The end of concern. We can't get the sand out of our eyes.

"There was a méchant man," I tell him, "who hated Africa and was covered in it."

He shakes his head. "You are not normal," he says. "And now you've cut your hair again. And unevenly at that. I think you're going a little crazy."

"No, I haven't cut my hair. I've just tied it back. Regarde."

"Yes. And you look a little crazy."

She begs for him and he likes it today. He likes her seductive stories. He can't pull himself away, and he's punishing her for it. As Lola has punished her.

She tries to imagine a self that does not yearn. A changeless, a final, a permanent self.

"I want you."

"Non."

He watches her watching her favorite waitress. "Why don't you go with her?" he says.

"I want you."

"Non. Ce n'est pas vrai."

He never says anything she wants to hear—not in French, not in English.

In the end Lola always said what she wanted. She followed her too closely. She cared too much about her ever-changing moods. She thought she could do something for a sadness that had nothing to do with anyone or anything. She felt as if she was failing when the woman was not happy.

But I was rarely happy in that way.

The depressed woman remembers how lucid she felt right after orgasm. How the depression lifted. How life for one moment seemed truly livable. It's not meant to be an excuse.

"I want you. Je te veux," she says. He's not responsible for anything. He starts to correct her French, but then stops.

"Non. Ce n'est pas possible. Je m'amuse. Je suis seul."

But she knows that he will not be able to stay away for long. He wants her to beg for him. She doesn't mind.


7


He draws me a map of his country on the table of the bar, and I draw him a map of mine.

He knows Téxas, Californie, Floride. It causes him some pain that he does not know where Maine is. "Alors—"

He shows me Nîmes, Bilot, Limoges, Nancy, Lourdes.

"Lourdes?" I say. "Perhaps I will go there to live."

"Non," he says, and he crosses it out. "Here is the Camargue."

"Oui," I say. "There are flamingos there. There are wild horses. They are born brown and they turn white as in a dream.

"And out there in the middle of the vast nowhere, with all the birds and the marshes and the rice and wild horses, is one small tabac. And next to it there is one newspaper stand and at the newspaper stand there is one *Nice-Matin*. And guess what the headline says?"

"What?"

"Michael Jackson—le concert de l'année."

He laughs. "I hate that story.

"You are a strange person," he says.

"And next to the Camargue is Arles. I have been to Arles."

"Quand?"

"A long time ago. A few months ago. I took a train," I tell him. "On the train there were cages. I sat in a cage full of German men who gazed out at the Méditerranée the whole time to Marseille. When they looked at me, as they did now and then, their blue eyes were still filled with sea and they softened for a moment. I am like their women, I know.

"Everywhere here you can still feel the war," I say.

He thinks about this.

"They are young Germans," I say. "They did not choose to be. In Arles I saw a horse that came up to my waist. A petit cheval. Clouds of white butterflies. A mutton with a mohawk."

"Comment?"

"A mutton shaved like an American Indian."

"Je ne comprends pas."

"I took a room on La Place du Docteur Pomme, where I went to get well. One hundred years ago Van Gogh walked there. I saw enormous squares of sunflowers that could make you go blind. Cigales so loud you could go deaf. Bright red dragonflies. I met a young Arlesian woman. It was her birthday. We ate the most delicious figs. White lights were strung across the square for the summer fêtes. I sang her the birthday song. She was eighteen that year."

"This year, you mean."

"Yes. We walked through town. We passed posters that said Exposition Internationale Féline—les plus beaux chats du monde."

"You are lovely," he says.

"Christian Lacroix was there. He had come home to show his fashions in the Arènes. There were bullfights. Some nights we could smell blood. Over the doorway of a bar, a single neon ear. Van Gogh lived here.

"We saw a Gypsy family. A father in a black vest was holding a llama on a leash. The mother had a tiny pony the size of a big poodle, and the little girl held the hand of a chimpanzee wearing blue shorts and a white shirt with umbrellas on it, sneakers, no socks. They kept walking up and down the main street of Arles, asking for money for giving us such a sight. People pressed and stared. 'They do this all day,' the patron of the bar said. Later we saw all of them out back behind a tiny mobile home.

"At night over a loudspeaker somewhere the same passage of music played over and over. The director with a microphone, a Godardian fellow orchestrating the scene, dancing between the ruins."

I tell him about the dark Arlesian on the white bed. The way her hips rose. "She had a triangular back."

"Back?"

"Dos. She wore a bloodred robe."

We look back at our map of the world. "Where is Mississippi?" he says.

I laugh.

"You are lovely," he says again, putting his hand over my country. I move it into the ocean. I draw a small circle.

"What is that?" he asks.

"Block Island. It was a place I once thought I could live."

"C'est très petit, non?" He smiles.

"Oui."

"Block Island." It sounds brutal in his mouth.

"I went there once in the American summer."

"Pour vacance?"

"Oui."

"Where is it that they make cars?"

"Here," I say, guiding his finger back to Michigan.

"What is the name?"

"Detroit."

"Oui," he says. "C'est ça! Detroit. And where is the fire?"

"What fire?"

He stares at me. "You don't know about the fire?" He can't believe it. He reports that all summer an enormous fire has raged out of control in the United States. In a national park. What is the name of the park, he wants to know.

"I don't know."

"Yes you do. It's a very big park," he says in English. "In the middle of the country. The pompiers can't put it out. Reagan says it is a natural fire." He laughs.

He shows me his favorite regions of France. He shows me where he likes to ski. Where he would go fishing. "What is the name in America for the big fish that fights? We do not have that fish here."

"A swordfish, maybe," I say. "I used to fish with my older brother."

"Oui? Do you like to fish?"

"Yes," I tell him. "I caught a trout once. We ate it on a terrace in the bright sun."

He catches la truite too, le brochet and a large black fish that lives only in France. "Have you thought of the name yet?"

"The name of what?"

"The name of the park?"

"Non."

In the center of my country he draws flames.

## 8

It's almost midnight, but her light is on.

"Oh," she says when she opens the door. "I quite like you as a Boy Scout!"

I'm wearing a blue scarf.

"Do come in."

She's chuckling, holding her notebook, remembering *a most amusing story!*

"I was just writing it down. I was in London, only a few years ago, and I was listening to a very interesting radio program, all about women, and suddenly there was an announcement. A woman got on and said, 'Because we can no longer say "lesbian" on the air, from now on we will refer to lesbians as "the women in comfortable shoes." ' " She laughs. "Oh, that's good! Don't you think? How Monica and I loved that one!

"You *will* stay for a nightcap?"

I nod.

I ask her about the French school system. I want to picture him as a petit. I want to see him tonight through every grade.

But she wants me to be faithful to her, though nothing has occurred.

"Oh," she says, sitting down with the bottle of gin and the bottle of tonic. "But quite a bit *has* occurred, my dear."

She tells me about the woman she loved who always lived with another woman. "And I of course was living with Monica. But we had a lovely little flirtation. Through the post. We had to have a code because our partners too would read the letters. So we devised words which we would use to let each other know we were thinking of the other. Her word was 'moon.' She would write, 'There is such a full moon tonight shining in my window, I can scarcely sleep!' And my word was 'morning.' 'A beautiful morning,' I wrote her, 'like no other.' "

Words once meant a great deal; I know that.

"Perhaps we should have code words. Let's see: I'd like

'midnight,' I think. Yes. Midnight."

Words once stood for something. Of course.

"Quite a bit has occurred, my dear."

"Your word," she says, "could be 'stars.'"

She thinks of Monica and herself laughing in front of the radio. She is seventy-five. In love with everything that's over. That's ending.

"I've got to leave now, Sylvia," I say. She knows where I'm going.

"But it's almost midnight, my dear. And look how beautiful the stars are."

"No, Sylvia, there are clouds. You can't see any stars tonight."

"Are you sure? Look closely."

"Yes, I'm sure."

"They are there," she smiles, "even if you can't see them."

"I know," I tell her.

I kiss her and get up to meet him.


# 9

They look out the window at the red sign that says PSYCHIC. She thinks of her older brother several streets away in a white room. He is dying.

She predicts now: "You will leave me for someone else. She'll be younger than we are. Simpler. Happy. More hopeful. She'll be someone who can drive, who likes to chat."

Lola laughs. Bats me away. Says, "You are crazy."

"No. She'll walk with her feet on the earth. In the real world. She'll be faithful. She'll be someone you don't have to worry about."

"I will never leave you," Lola says, "even though you are a pain."

"You will. She'll be nice. She'll like to cook."

"Really?" Lola says. "And what about you?"

I shrug. "I feel the ending of all things," I say.

"It is because of your older brother."

"I see a future of only limits."

"Don't be silly," Lola says. "I will always love you. I will love you forever. I will never leave you."

I smile.

They are sitting in the small, in the dark, in the city, staring at the red sign that says PSYCHIC.


## 10


He never wants to hear about the men, and there have been many men. He never asks anything about them.

He really only wants to know about the one I cry for. He'll listen about the others too.

"But not the men. OK?"

I am still known as the American woman in the Chinese hat who writes and who cries. Sometimes the people of this village can see the dazzling and doomed city in my eyes, where young people, my friends, get lost, or leave, or die.

Over the radio at the bar: "Don't leave me this way."

Still there was a great deal I loved about my city. I think of the last time I was there. The light on the Twin Towers.

"I miss home," I tell him. "I miss many things," I say, but I wonder if it's true.

He nods.

I tell him that I have talked to my mother. I tell him she doesn't like me to be in France because it is so far away. He says, "Tell her to come here and live near you."

"Look at that girl over there," I say.

"Which one?"

"The one with the real short hair and red lipstick eating a little mouse made out of chocolate. The one with the red shirt and red sandals."

"What about her?"

"Nothing."

She notices how gradually everything is turning red.

"That man over there—"

"Oui?"

"He is an American composer. But he no longer composes."

She notices how gradually everything is surrendered or thrown away.

She recalls the Chinese emperor standing in front of the sink and how the water turned red.

"One summer," I tell him, "a girl reads *Death in Venice,* on a beach. She picks up a pen every now and then and writes 'important' in the margins. She puts a question mark next to the part about Aschenbach's fear of being ridiculous; for what could be ridiculous in his pure search for beauty?"

"I don't understand what you're saying. Speak French."

"Ce n'est pas important," I say.

Some years later I will love the young woman who writes notes in that book, I think. "I pity that young girl who one day will have to endure a long list of crimes—the great ones, the small ones too."

"You're saying strange things tonight," he says.

"There was once a man," I say.

"Not the man, please."

"Yes. There was once a man," I tell him, "who left a swastika on my neck."

"You are folle."

"It's true. He was in the Front National. He was from around here."

"How did he leave that on your neck?"

"She let him. Even though she detested him. Maybe because she detested him. Tu comprends, Lucien?"

"Non."

"Tu comprends rien."

It's the self-loathing that's so hard, I think, in the time after her.

"In the desert, she tried to scream."

"What desert?"

"In the red desert with the man with the swastika."

"Why did you say swastika?"

She shrugs. Sighs.

Once it would have meant something. She tries to remember detesting that man. She's losing interest in her own anger. She's becoming bored of Clover too, even Lola, though she never imagined it would be possible.

"I told you I didn't want to hear about the men."

"I forgot. I'm sorry. I don't feel at home here," I say.

"Of course not," he says. "What did you think?"

We are sitting in the Place du Peyra today, where four thousand years ago blood poured down these streets right under our feet. Place of leaf and shadow. Small and large crimes. Ancient hatreds. Human emotion. Stone.


## 11

Again, she says: "I thought you said it never rained here in summer."

She asks him the difference between "oui" and "whey," which is how most people say "oui" here. She asks him to teach her more slang. He looks at the book on her night table. He laughs. *The History of French Civilization.*

"What part are you up to?"

"Jeanne d'Arc."

He laughs again. "You have a long way to go."

"Not so far," she says dreamily.

"Oui."

"Whey" is like "yeah."

There is the excitement of rain after having no rain for a long time. "I thought you told me it never rained in summer."

"Après le quinze août, il pleut." He laughs. He's caught me believing something he has said. Fool, he thinks.

The sound of rain after no rain.

"The ville is all pink and peach," she says. "The tomb is covered with roses."

"What color?"

"Yellow.

"There are billboards. Nino Cerutti. Yves St. Laurent. Women in expensive clothes. Perfume hangs in the air.

"There's a gigantic Wasserly. Candles. An incredible blue-lit casino."

"It's Monaco!" he says, delighted.

"The chiming of the palace clock. La Centre de Jeunesse Princesse Stéphanie. Lycée Albert 1er. Avenue Princesse Grace."

They make love once, twice. The rain beats on the tile roof. "Are you sure you didn't see that film?" she asks sleepily. "Bruno Ganz was an angel."

"Yes, I am sure," he whispers, petting her head. And I am moved again by this tenderness. This place, despite everything, that opens in him.

"Did you ever see that Alfred Hitchcock movie? Grace Kelly and Cary Grant. . . ."

The smell of lovemaking and rain. "You said it never rained here—"

"Après le quinze août, oui, whey—" He's drifting off.


12

We try to keep talking while above us Tourrettes burns.

Ma forêt c'est sacrée.

Once you see one fire here you begin to understand this people's obsession with fire. It's the end of a season, a season without fire, until now. It's been hot. It could have been spontaneous combustion. It could have been anything.

"J'ai peur, Lucien."

From the sky all summer fire retardant had been spread. Now the mistral starts up. The wind here named for a poet, the wind now that spreads fire. Breath of a poet.

We look out past the line of trees and there are flames. The sound of the pompiers in the distance.

She remembers the summer where she tried to lose herself in smoke of all kinds, in the smoky purple grapes, in the mushrooms that tasted like smoke in this forest-fire region.

"The name of the park," she says. "It is Yellowstone."

"C'est ça!"

Something is burning in the distance.

Love me.

"I am your last dream," he whispers. "Le dernier rêve."

One asks for just a few more days.

The fire burns out of control. Or so it seems.

"There is nothing we can do about it," he says. "There is nothing we can do to make it stop."

She remembers the summer she tried to lose herself in smoke. She cries, and he watches her cry.


13


She cries and he watches her cry. He feels as if he is losing his mind. He gets up to leave. His hair turning a moment after the turn of his exquisite head.

"Dix chats sauvages," she says in slow-motion.

He turns back. "Qu'est-ce que tu as dit?"

"Dix chats sauvages," she says, as if they were with her in that room.

"Maybe in the beginning it wasn't as many as dix," she says. "Trois ou peut-être quartre. He gave them milk—the little boy. And bricolage from his father's market."

"Pas bricolage," Lucien says.

"But every day there were more and more chats sauvages. No one could explain it. No one really cared. But it became a little strange, a little bizarre after a while. All these chats crying and crying.

"Sometimes," she says, "when there was nothing else, he would feed them his sandwich jambon or his croque-monsieur."

"Je pense que non," Lucien says.

"Si, c'est vrai. Dix chats sauvages. He's only a little boy. He counts them over and over."

"Quelle couleur?" Lucien asks.

"Noir," she says. "Ten black cats. Ten solitary creatures asking for food, crying all the time. He loves them. He feels like he understands them. These mysterious creatures. He tries to make a cage for them. But they always escape.

"One day he finds a sack just large enough to fit dix chats sauvages. He carefully puts them all in the sack and, it's terrible, but he drowns them in the water."

"Non!"

"Si, c'est vrai."

"Mais pourquoi?"

She shrugs. "They would never stop crying. Or maybe he hated that they ran away. C'est triste, n'est-ce pas?"

"Mais pourquoi?" he asks again. "C'est terrible!"

She thinks it's possible he has not understood her story. She can't tell what he's understanding.

"They were crying too much," she says. She rubs up against him, pushing her head into his chest. "Tout le temps. Nuit et jour." She purrs.

He watches her take off her clothes. Slowly she moves toward him. He thinks she is perhaps the softest thing he has ever touched. But tonight he just stares.

"Nuit et jour. So much crying. And he can't bear it. He can't stand it anymore. And they're so hungry and homesick."

He trembles.

"He just wants them to be silent. She rubs her head down his chest. Her eyes gleam.

"Feed me," she whispers. "J'ai faim."

"Comme toujours," he says.

"There was no other choice," she says. "J'ai faim," she whispers, licking him with hunger.

He pulls away. He does not dare touch her.


## 14


"She enters this scene weeping," I tell him. "She makes a list of all the things she's afraid of: white asparagus, pâté, a black swan, bats, the entire country of India, the beggars with the signs that say 'pour manger,' the city of Berlin." She shudders. "She'd like to devour everything she's afraid of for dinner. Dix chats sauvages."

"You are not normal."

"With the woman I despaired at the limits of words, paint, musical notes."

The limits of love.

"You are bizarre," he says. "Pourquoi Berlin?"

The evening evaporates in wine. "I'm afraid of everything some nights. Of even the memory of the bodies of cows on a road, or a white room, or a red dress."

"Qu'est-ce que tu as dit?"

"Et les chauve-souris, that's bald mice, that's bats in English, and who wouldn't be?

Arabic music snakes through the old town. Little Moroccan children pick up the rice after weddings and I am afraid. How the evening dissolves in wine.

She spoke of death by suffocation. She wondered why she dreamt such things.

"And now I have a stomachache too."

"Pourquoi?"

"Because on the way here I ate all the blackberries off the bushes."

He closes his eyes. "You are strange. You seem to have stopped drinking," he says. "I still don't believe it." He never trusted her.

"But you did, you started to believe me. You felt shame about the cats."

He's had enough.

She tells him a story: "It is already night when she goes there. The black water of the fountain still flows. The full moon hurts them—is hurting them.

" 'Where have you been,' he asks. The young man stares into black water.

" 'I have been to London to see the queen. No,' she says gravely, 'I have been to visit the yearning man in the white bed. He gave me dark fruit. I thought forever.' "

He turns to me. "C'est fini," he whispers. "She is completely crazy."

I feel the lateness of the century in his embrace.


## 15


"Je suis fatigué," he says. He drinks. He grows sullen. He's angry tonight, méchant. He writes "C'est nul," then "Zéro," in water on stone. He tries to think of an ending to all this. He writes "The End."

"Stop writing that, s'il vous plaît."

"S'il *te* plaît," he corrects her.

"What is it, Lucien?"

"Oh, when you are done with this place you'll go somewhere else. When you're done with me, you'll leave, find someone else. When the book is finished—"

But there will be no book.

He writes "Fin." He tries to think of a way out of this.

Maybe there could be a story. But he doubts it.

"Listen," I say. "Écoute. Closely. Lucien.

"She walks down the Promenade des Anglais. One more time she admires the Negresco. That palace by the sea. Most of Neptune Plage is closed. It's where she went one day with a young American poet." It seems long ago.

"It's the end of a season. In the stores the signs say 'Fin de Series.'"

He listens hard. Drinks.

Bernard Henri-Lévy's new book is just out: *Les Derniers jours de Charles Baudelaire*. It's in every window.

"Oui, B. H. L.," he says.

"At a café a woman arches her back the better to see into the hand mirror she holds. She calls for the garçon in her singsong voice. There's no real life for women here. That much seems clear.

"The French wear sweaters over their T-shirts that say GOLF CLUB and BOWLING TEAM and SURF. SURF.

"The tide pulls back. There is nothing but stones.

"'So many blue chairs in Nice,' she says to herself. She closes her eyes to feel one last time the heat and the breeze. . . ."

"C'est tout?"

"Non. She takes the bus back to Vence. On the way home, she stops at the cemetery.

"She walks down the aisles of raised graves. She passes the small photographs of the dead. She passes porcelain flowers, roses floating in their glass globes in this land of roses. She reads the inscriptions: 'Ici repose François Giraud. Regrets éternels.' 'A mon cher Papa.' And 'Marie Barriere. Notre mère adorée.'"

I thought she'd always be there.

"'Ici repose Boyer, Anne Marie, née Chaubert.' She walks down aisle after aisle of the dead and weeps.

"'Ici, Paul Emile, à notre ange et frère regretté 1931-32.'

"I remember the day the sirocco came. 'You have the kind of ankles women had before the war,' the man said."

I had wanted to grow old with her. Silly of me. Today I'm not sure I'll grow old at all.

We loved the Hôtel Rivoli on the rue Pastorelli in Nice. She drew me a map of Nice once.

"She looks at the small gravestone in front of her. It says: 'A mon époux et papa chéri. Victime de la barbarie nazie.' She weeps."

She thinks this is how life is. She thinks about how at the last moment you were always asked to give up one more thing.

I am forced here to fully imagine what life will be like without her. There is no consolation. This was the day she should have arrived; but there's someone else now.

"She leaves the cemetery. She walks into the market. There are snails in a cage. Vin rosé. Wind. A lowering source of light."

He nods his head. "The light of septembre is la plus belle," he says. The most beautiful.

"One last thing. On the way back from town she remembers the funerary urn she once saw at the archaeological museum by the sea. Do you know what it says?"

He shakes his head, "Non."

"It says: 'To the spirit of Septentrion—twelve years—who danced at the Antibes Theatre for two days and was a success.' "

She takes his hand.


16


The light of septembre is la plus belle, he tells her. And he is right.

She remembers one more time: catching fish.

She remembers: her father in the garden with his magnifying glass.

She remembers: in the dark city they drank grappa.
The light on the Twin Towers.
She was sure somehow that they'd always be together.
He says the September light is the most beautiful.
How fragile we were!
I remember the great city. I know that once we were happy there. Film school. CBGB. No deadly disease.
Many things are difficult for him; he's said that. He's writing me letters he'll never send. He's told me that in advance.
Écrire is to write. Souvenir is to remember. Arrêter, I know, is to stop.
There are no rules for what is a masculine noun and what is a feminine noun. You just have to learn them by heart.
I don't know where we ever got the idea that a few fish would be enough. I don't know what we were thinking—after all we'd been through.
Arrêter is to stop. Elle s'arrête: She stops. She stops now.
I walk into the Friday market. From a table I pick up a door knocker in the shape of a woman's hand. It is French. It is from the time of la belle époque.
You would have liked it here.
I buy the door knocker in the shape of a woman's hand for my mother. I hand the money to the man. I smile. I've even learned to spend the centimes.
It was silly to think we could have lived on olive oil, tomatoes, a few small fish.
Still.
Still, if you had come: we would have drunk wine from La Gaude and Saint-Jeannet. We would have eaten the figs.
Retrouver is to find again.
A few figs in a dish. Artichaut violets. We thought it might be enough once.
September. One remembers all the changes from warmth to coolness. One remembers every change in degree or commitment or intention and weeps.
September and the tuna move into the bay. My waitress is going back to school in Paris.

The light of septembre is la plus belle, he says.

Gone in an instant the *Jean de Florette* heat of summer.

The imperfect tense is used when an action that began in the past was interrupted and remains incomplete.

She remembers how they tried to tell stories through the dazzling silence.

She remembers how they practiced tenir and revenir in the white room.

How beautiful she would have looked tanned under a white umbrella at La Régence in the last days of summer. I can almost taste her nutty skin.

One wants to begin to trust again—even the trompe l'œil. The deceptive, perfect surface.

I might have made her a paper-napkin hat. We might have tried to guess the nationalities of the people at the next tables. We might have made up the stories of their lives. We could have pretended she was Basque.

We would have torn off the ends of a baguette. Admired the fall fashions. Put a tint in her long hair.

I would have liked to have taken a photo of her in this light. She would have looked lovely here, I know.


## 17


She imagines two women who have lived together for forty years. Their eyes haze over and they stare somewhat blankly when the other speaks, not because they are bored, but because they love each other too much. And one must begin to say good-bye, sometime.

A fierce wind. I hear Sylvia yelling in the distance: "We'll all be blown to bits!"

When I get to her she's safely inside the mas called Paradis and she is holding her notebook. "Sylvia!"

"It's pandemonium!"

I tell her I am leaving soon. That I've come to say good-bye for now.

She's been writing in her notebook. "You'll have to excuse me," she says, "for just a minute."

I remember watching the Chinese emperor and how everything turned red.

In the other room she rereads to herself a poem she has written about her beloved Monica from the fallen empire of L, dead now ten years.

Lola said: love. Lola said: forever.

"Listen," she says.

It is so lovely, so filled with longing for what she once had. For what I once had. Rain, this September day. Tears.

She is speaking her refined English as we look out over the French countryside, missing everything.

Everyone says you are happy, Lola. Everyone says you are happy finally. It is something.

I don't know what we could have been thinking—that a few figs would have been enough. A handful of words. When there was so much ocean.

More than anything I had wanted to write. To say something. To live with you and be safe. To fill the silence for a moment.

I look at Sylvia, small, holding her notebook. "My Monica," she says. She trembles.

I had done Sylvia—this woman whom I had so admired, even loved—a disservice. I had turned her into a character. I saw that now. A literary invention. I had imposed a false shape on her. I had diminished her in an attempt to understand something about my life. I had been in need of comfort, in need of consolation. I had invented her to give me courage, to ease my pain. For who was the real Sylvia, after all?

"I'm sorry," I say now. "I'm sorry for everything." I wanted to fill something that can never be filled. I see that now.

"Don't be sorry," she says. She takes my hand. "Before you go, I want to give you a cutting of banksia," she whispers.

"It's an early rose without thorns."

We walk into the greenhouse. Outside: wind, rain.

"There's such a hush," she says. "How curious."

She is strangely wordless.

I do not even allow myself to think that I will never see her again.

"It's very curious. All these feelings. After so long. Tears, tears," she says quietly, her hands fluttering around her face.

I give up for good the notion that I could ever be like her. That she is some future, cherished version of myself.

She squeezes my hand. "You'll be back," she says. "And please, dear Catherine, when you come, don't forget your comfortable shoes."

## 18

These are the tentative last days of summer. The pool begins to empty. The splashing girls and boys. The pushing and running children.

"Attendez," she says out loud. "A few more days."

Why must things end?

No use assigning blame. That much they can agree on. That much seems right. It's over, that's all.

Choisir is to choose.

She watches one more wedding: the large cars, the extravagant flowers, the carriage and horses, the bride and groom. And then all disappears, the hundreds of guests, the cars. The Moroccan children come, pick up the scattered rice and put it in bags.

One says good-bye slowly or not at all. She walks into the cathedral, into its consuming darkness, its small lights, its offrandes. Its bleeding, its most sacred heart at the altar in a box.

She would never understand what made her weep this

way. Or why she could not stay. Or why she could no longer become the Virgin. Or pray.

The light fades. Pas encore, I think. Not yet.

Cloudy drinks. A white bird. A plane tree leaf falls.

The long shadows cast on this page at La Régence, as the sun sets.

There's no getting beyond the surface, that much is clear. It's the surface I love. What I can see. Perfect light. What I can touch. Marble. Hard and gleaming. Cool in the heat. And a hand running under water. Words lost in rushing water and a red dress. How we hurried. Hurry.

I watch the young at every table talking under white umbrellas. I'll never understand what they say.

"Have you seen Lucien?" I ask my favorite waitress.

"No," she smiles. She's beautiful in her flowered dress. Across the square, music, wine, lights. "Maybe," she says, "he is dancing."

## 19

Rain this day. The rafts on display outside the sporting-goods store, floating all summer through the heat of Vence, now deflated.

The great expensive cars that have hovered all season around town go back to Paris or wherever it is they have come from. I don't see the children or the small dogs or the women getting in. I just notice that one day they are no longer here. Their sleek, chic bodies leave, the press of their money, their tans. It is really OK with the people of Vence—Paris is a bother and now that they have made their money for the season, they'd just as soon go back to not remembering it.

Les Floralies, Les Charmettes, La Mignonette, Sans Souci, Le Mas Rose—all empty now.

Along the road I count the figs that have fallen to the ground. So many figs. One hundred. Two hundred.

Everything grows quiet. Empty. It's the off-season she embraces. The open spaces, the rain.

My American friends pack to leave. I smile when they show me the souvenirs they've bought. All the photos they took of the food they ate. I realize I don't understand them. Perhaps I never did.

"Come back with us to your real life," they say.

I look at them strangely. "What real life?"

She thinks they walk through France unscathed and she is fascinated by it.

I assure them that I'll be home soon. Kiss them good-bye. Once, twice on the cheeks.

Lola has written that she is coming to get me if I do not return soon. Lola writes: "You cannot stop me. No one owns France, Catherine, not even you."

Joan of Arc owns France. Joan of Arc.

Lola writes: love. And I love you. Lola writes: let's try again. She can't live without me. Strange. But who can believe in love anymore?

I think of a woman's dark hair growing long in another country, a country called home.

Who can believe what the American friends are now saying? Words meant something once. American. Friend. They say: Lola is coming next Sunday at twelve if you do not come now. They say: love. They say that affair is over.

She remembers lying on their bed. Her arms pinned behind her like wings.

She remembers now weeping at the limits of things.

Come home with us now, the American friends say. But who can believe any of it? She looks up suddenly. "I dreamed of you both the other night," she says, waving at them through rain as they get smaller and smaller and farther and farther, "and that we were friends again."

And it is they now who are weeping. Strange ones. A French song on the radio. She can't quite make out the words. No matter. I think it must be beautiful. Filled with innocence, yearning, something hopeful.

I think of her far away in our real country—sitting on a beach, understanding the words with someone new, her life beginning again.

When it is three o'clock here it is only nine in the morning there.

I don't know why no one picked the figs.

## 20

My favorite waitress, the one who said  Maybe he is dancing,' comes dressed in black and white silk pants, a midriff top; her shift starts at eleven. She is beautiful again today.

Tenir. Tenir is to hold. These months suddenly gone.

Let her hold them all here once more. The people of the pâtisseries, the butchers, the pompiers. The young at La Victoire, and the Bambou, and La Régence. Vence Fleurs. Parasols. Les fruits, les légumes. Let her hold them one more moment. The marbled European cats. The old, aging in this place ten kilometers from the sea. Church bells ring. The women haul wooden crates. Everything begins to close for déjeuner. She holds these streets she's memorized: the rue du Marché, avenue de la Résistance, the Place Antony Mars.

This man by the fountain.

"Lucien!"

He smiles. Kisses her twice on the cheeks.

Brilliance of the afternoon. There's no way past the surface. She'll never get beyond it. She'll never understand anything. It's easier to see in another country.

Ce soir, I tell him, is the Festin Ravioli. He shakes his head.

Not to forget the light. One expects the light to fade but it doesn't. It continues to caress everything with its even-handed justice. The glasses of wine. The Tunisians. The crucified Christ. The poodles.

One feels the imminent departure of the favorite waitress. The dogs. I think I will even miss the silly dogs.

I think of the slightly mournful Ravioli Festival, the mark of the season's end.

We walk to my stone house. I am eating the last blackberries.

"They are not the last," Lucien says.

"Oui, the last for me."

"Reste ici," he says. "Stay here. The light of septembre is la plus belle. The most beautiful. Stay."

I never got to Fréjus. I never got to Mougins or Cannes.

No one really understands this—why this cannot be. But it cannot.

It should have been possible, I think, to have gotten by with the present tense. To have thrived somehow on the dazzling surface.

We walk for a long time. Pass the Chapelle du Rosaire with its rose light.

So many red leaves—like feet.

These fragile days. She counts the figs. No more the hunger for figs. The hunger for an arrangement of anything.

Vin rosé. Côtes du Rhône. So many roses—and a red dress.

Again he notices: "You seem to have stopped drinking." He doesn't believe it.

"Drinking clouds the feeling of the end," she says. "Drinking obscures the obvious implications of the trompe l'œil." Drinking clouds the loss of everything, she thinks.

"Why did you say 'trompe l'œil'?" She laughs. She still can't stop thinking.

They walk further. The green vines redden. In fall, she remembers, he was one of the catastrophically, the desperately ill. She closes her eyes. The little Chinese emperor says, "Ouvrez la porte."

## 21

She recalls the walls of the Forbidden City. Pulls him toward her. He looks at her smooth arm. Holds it tightly now.

"Do you remember that story about Madame Butterfly?" She holds an imaginary knife in the air. "And the way the water turned red?"

He is being drawn in against his will, and irresistibly. "Come to bed," he whispers.

"It is très, très chaud. Dark curtains fall to the floor. All night wheat is being scythed. A knife is near the bed. She's standing at the sink running her wrists under cool water. It is the Rhône, say. And there is a war on." She shrugs. "Or there is no war."

"Is there a war or not?"

"It doesn't really matter," she whispers. "The American woman in the Chinese hat—"

"Oui?"

"She is going away."

"I knew it all along," he whispers. "Where?"

"Maybe to China."

"Why China?"

She remembers a little emperor huge on a wall in a room in France. Made of light.

"That was a film," Lucien says.

"It was a complicated story. It was hard to understand in French." She cries.

"Come to bed."

"The American woman in the Chinese hat—"

"Oui?"

"She's not American at all. She is German, maybe, or suédoise. She has no hat. And she has no notebook. The American woman who writes."

"But why?" he asks.

"She wanted to be a mermaid or a dolphin or a bird. But she couldn't."

"Come to bed."

For a last moment she is able to sum up the extraordinary vastness just outside the town where wheat is being scythed, the dark Rhône flowing like wine now near the large bed. I give her this—the cigales—can you hear them pulsing against the night—as she moves gracefully into the end, wearing it like a dark crown.

And she is grateful. All along she has been grateful. For the beautiful Arlesian. For the fountain. For the friends. For the man. For this:

It is a rented room in Arles when the sun comes back after an afternoon of lovemaking. She tries to make sense of something. They drink a little Côtes du Rhône next to the Rhône in a rented room in Arles. She cries a little. There is bread and cheese. Wine, which she needs. A knife.

She's standing at the sink running her wrists under cool water. She turns to her. Touches the ghost horse of her body.

"You are still the same as you were then," I say to the young Arlesian. "So beautiful. . . . But the room—it seems different. I don't remember the knife from before. Or your bloodred robe."

"No," she whispers. "Everything is the same. It is you who have changed."

Red. Rhône. Fish. Figs. "How was it we tired even of the figs?"

I look again. Still there is a room. A knife. A woman in a red robe I wish I could love.

"Tell me another story," Lucien begs.

"She touches the walls of the Forbidden City—"

"Not the little emperor again."

"OK, OK," she says. "There were two sisters," she tells him. "Once upon a time there were two sisters, Cheveux d'Ange and Papillon."

" 'Cheveux d'Ange and Papillon'?"

"Oui."

He thinks for a moment, then laughs. "Those aren't the names of girls. Those are the names—" and he tries to think of the word in English, "of spaghettis."

"No interrupting, Lucien," I say.

"Cheveux d'Ange and Papillon sit at La Victoire. All the birds fly from the plane tree at the same time. Someone in the square puts on *Madame Butterfly* and they cry."

"Non," he says, "not another sad story. Non. I will tell you a story," he says.

"Oui?"

"La femme américaine—" he says.

"Oui?"

"She stays here. En France."

"Vraiment? Pourquoi?"

"There are many things to write."

"Like what?"

"How it feels to open the shutters for the first time. One side of the book will be in English and the other side in French."

"Oui?"

"She will learn French history. She is still on Jeanne d'Arc. She has a long way to go."

"Not so far," I say.

"Yes. Far."

"I like the story you tell about that woman."

"She goes to la Bataille des Fleurs," he says. "She dances in the square."

"Avec qui?"

"Avec . . . avec Cheveux d'Ange."

"Angel Hair," she whispers, pulling him close. "Cheveux d'Ange."

He trembles.

They are losing their way—it is plain to see.

"Non," he says. "Elle danse toute seule."

She sees a man folding a woman over a brilliant window. She looks out at the roses. She felt like a bird once.

## 22

I am losing the ability to dream her, to make her up—this lovely construction of self. The stories had said: I exist. Even when they were sad. It was something. The stories were shelter for a while. Company.

I was hoping to tame my terror with sex or language, to bear the solitude with stories or—

Love is what is dangerous under the bright surface of saluts and ça vas and many-colored drinks. Under the polka-dotted umbrellas and bells.

He holds a shining green bottle. Brings it up to his lips, in light. Vittel.

She walks through the agony of the afternoon to him. He is standing next to the fountain. She smiles. Waves. I am the American woman in the Chinese hat who waves. Who writes. Who wrote once. He comes forward. So much silence maintenant.

She thought that love might—as the songs from America said.

Once she thought this: she in the Chinese hat. He with his cheveux longs. That it was enough. Once there was a little horse—once a hotel— No.

We loved the Hôtel Rivoli. One night by the sea. And the green freedom of a cockatoo.

I touch his cheek. "You are beautiful, beautiful."

She's singing, off-key. He covers his ears.

> "Row, row, row your boat
> Gently down the stream
> Merrily, merrily, merrily, merrily,
> Life is but a dream."

He sings: Merrily, merrily, merrily, merrily. . . .

We tried to speak in the savage and beautiful afternoon and couldn't anymore. And in the night. He said, "Dix chats sauvages."

He whispers, "Life is but a dream," off-key.

When it is five o'clock here, in this room, trying to remember wanting, trying to remember you, it is—what time is it there?

Dimanche and the bells.

I do not think you will think to look for me here.

She is locked, as he whispers and sings, sings in a whisper, in his perfect, amoral face. But she can't live there. And she can't live anywhere else either.

Everyone here is kissing everyone else, once, twice, on the bright, the dazzling, luminous surface.

She tries to call it up, what she must have felt once about him: you are beautiful like a girl.

The Vence regulars come and go. Names I would hope someday to know.

She tries to hold on. But everything begins to slip. If she could only talk to them about lipsticks or figs.

I loved you once, and the world was a cathedral of light—surely you have not forgotten. I look at her with my blind eye.

Everyone is sitting under white umbrellas drinking their drinks, tossing their heads, talking.

She mimics the living now: picks up a drink. Eats a little. Cries for the one mercifully dead. Mercy.

Waiters glide by. And on the radio Sade still sings about Paradise.

Love should be like this: the exquisite young man, standing by the fountain at the end. A luminous stream of water flowing.

Each word a boat.

"Cheveux longs" she had written in her notebook. In the beautiful forever of the afternoon. She thinks of Aschenbach.

One feels on the verge of fluency.

And then suddenly not.

She remembers the days when he was bathed in amber and she called the world a cathedral of light. If there is any longing in her now, it is for that day.

## 23

She looks at him, her delirious and passionate guest.

She looks at him for a long time. She wonders whether they've really understood anything each other has said.

She touches his fragile and delicate face and tries to imagine forever.

"Tell me a story," he says. He closes his eyes and waits.

"Pour la prochaine fois," she says, exhausted. "A woman comes and sits at a bar. At the tables around a fountain." He smiles. "She orders a pastis. It comes in a tall glass that says 'Pastis 51.' She adds water from a carafe and it turns into a cloud in her glass."

He smiles.

"You finish it," she says. She can't help it. She starts to cry.

And I am seeing them from what seems far away and they are getting smaller and smaller, like midgets.

He speaks in French. He says, "And all the while a young man is watching and revolving his postcard racks that are outside the galerie where he works. She can almost feel him on her back as he slowly rotates the colorful cards. He comes and sits behind her. He is wearing a Kenzo T-shirt. She is writing in her notebook and he is so close that if he wanted to, he could see what she is writing."

"He makes her nervous," she says.

"Pourquoi nerveuse?"

"You know."

"Oui."

"She's got a shirt on with a very low-cut back," he says. "She's wearing a Chinese hat. It's hot and she can feel him staring at her. Then he gets up. Goes back to the place he was standing. He lights a cigarette. His straight hair falls in his face and he combs it back with his hand."

"In the window of his store there's a book: *L'Innocence des fleurs*," she says. They are fighting to stay in this.

"The patron at the Bar Marseillais has been watching the whole thing," he says.

"The young man, the one who is so beautiful, is leaning back now, his fingertips in the water as if he's part of the fountain. He turns and takes a drink," I say. "Viens. 'Come here,' she thinks.

"The sound of rushing water floods her. She looks up. He walks over.

"'Vous parlez français?' the young man asks. She lives in New York. He lives near the cemetery."

He doesn't want to hear the end. "It is 28 degrees in New York now," he says. "The same as here."

"Oui," she says. "The woman at the fountain, she is in awe, as if she is the witness to some last and perfect light."

"But the light will last," Lucien says, "even though you go." He turns away. "You will not come back."

"Si, je reviens."

"You have another life. Une autre vie." He thinks of the woman I have wept for all summer.

"No. That life is over. You do not understand."

The woman whose hair has grown now to the middle of her back—that far?—gets on a plane to France. Too late.

He tries to picture me far away in a huge city. "We don't say 'city' in French. There is no word for 'city.' We say 'ville.' " He wishes for one moment that there were a word for the place she's about to go.

She thinks of the young French man from the unmade film by the dead Truffaut.

She looks at the young French man she imagined she could die for. She tries to recall the enormity of her desire. What does she desire now? She studies him closely. She can think of nothing in this world.

With her hand she covers one eye. In this language there is no word for that city. She cries.

## 24

They pass the Peruvian band in the square. She tells him she remembers the Mexican dance hall. Green chairs lined up around the edge of the room. No. Non.

"The baron took a lover in every perched village from Eze to—"

"Oui?"

She sighs. There's not one story that will change this. That makes any sense. No beginning, no middle, no end. Most of all not a story like that.

So many blue chairs. Each word a fig.

They sit at the bar called Le Club. She looks around her in the perfect and fluent afternoon. People were talking. People were laughing. Understanding everything. She looks at him. His mobile and passionate head.

"I love you," she says, forcing it out. She blurts it out. He laughs.

"Oui," he says. "I am your hero."

His indifferent, detached head.

"Tell me something else," he says.

"No." It's not possible to come up with one true sentence, one arrangement of words that would mean anything

"One more story."

"That woman over there," I say. "Even though she lives in France, she still speaks Spanish in her sleep."

"Non, there's not one thing that you've told me that I believe," he says in French. "There's no story. It's only words."

She laughs. "And you don't understand them."

She points. It's the albino midget. They wave. He comes over and puts his arms around her. "You are my hero," she says.

He's got cocaine today. Heroin. "Do you want quelque chose?"

"Non," Lucien says. Drugs are for people who believe there is an escape. They are for people who think there's a solution, a way out of this. He laughs. In this moment they realize they want nothing in this world.

Once we thought our bodies might be birds or dolphins, or a boat. Once we thought— Everyone here is kissing.

The albino midget shakes his head. Lucien waves him away. Then shouts: "Dit non à la drogue."

Sometimes she thinks this is a story about living without consolation. Without shelter. It's not like we didn't try.

"Just say no," she says. We laugh at the stupidity of Nancy Reagan. How have I come to this, I wonder. Where am I?

She asks him to hurt her. To tie her. To make her bleed. To make her feel something. Once more.

He looks at her and laughs. "Non. Ce n'est pas possible."

She just wants to feel something.

She takes from her pocket the thin book with gold letters. Holds it in her palm and laughs in the dangerous afternoon. It's so small. Who has ever seen a book so small? She lights a match. "Ma forêt c'est sacrée," he says. "Attention," he says, laughing.

He reads "Passport." He reads "United States of America." It's so far.

She just wants to feel something. "Dit non à la drogue," she says as they watch the blue book burn, as she waves good-bye, as she slips out of this last credential of self.

Love: as the songs from America said.

"Where is your cahier?" She scares him, this American.

"Gone," she says. "All gone."

She takes off her hat. They stare at the singed and ruined book.

"You will stay then?" he whispers.

She laughs.

## 25

"Dear Catherine,

"It's still hot and humid here but I know fall is coming. Acorns are falling from the oak trees and there are bits of red on the dogwood leaves, the days are getting shorter and everywhere there are back to school sales. I'll be glad to see the fall come even though it's never been my favorite season. I think it's because you'll be back home, and the bad dreams I've been having about you will finally stop."

I try to imagine the woman who is called My Mother. Who writes me these things. I study the words she has assigned to everything. The way she choses to describe all the space between us.

It's so far. . . .

Friends say that Lola has married in a small church in a mountain village in France. Meaningful words were exchanged; rings.

My mother writes: It's hard for him to hear *Madame Butterfly*.

She is in love. I'm glad.

My mother writes there has been an accident. The eye has detached.

My older brother and I hold hands in the white room—and look out on a city on fire.

The child says: jeté.

He was listening to the wires that went into his ears.

He was deaf then, remember?

She notices how everything is thrown away.

The child says jeté now.

Friends say she is happy.

Once we thought love. Or the sad stories might. . . .

She puts her notebook away, acknowledging the limits of things.

She says: rose . . . boat . . .

Why must the world end?

She'll never understand.

Mais, quelque fois— In a different time—
She sewed me a tutu. Red feet. Those were mine.

She remembers the time they caught fish. Those fish were imaginary. No matter.

My mother has pretty handwriting. I love her. I wish she would come here.

## 26

The eye floats in its bag of water detached from the retina. She passes chinchillas in cages. Lambs and rabbits in their doomed stalls. Bicyclettes pass. Women with baguettes. Goats gambol around a dancing nymph. A whole way of life passes.

These fragile days.

The little girls wear plastic pool bracelets on their ankles.

L'étrangère, they all say.

There is no mistaking what this is. She hears a large, undeniable grief of bells. Flowers float in their watery globes.

This is good-bye.

I touch the American woman gently on the shoulder. She smiles at me. "You think we wouldn't have needed much."

She whispers to me, "It's OK." She whispers, "Thank you for everything. For the fruit, and the light, and the hat."

In the square, in the aimless afternoon, a boy blows through a reed flute, standing on one foot, on this lonely part of the planet called France. An animal skin is stretched over a barrel. That's what?—a drum. In French—she doesn't want to learn any more words.

At the cemetery roses float in their watery globes.

All those lights were people's lives.

They close the black book.

The young men erase their names. She reads blank pages. She passes Mary in blue, faceless and mute. She passes the attenuated Christ hanging, still suffering in the light of this day. Trapped in his body. Going nowhere.

My older brother with wires in his ears on this solitary planet.

She puts her cheek against his wooden foot.

The pulsing rose of his heart.

She sees a man folding a woman over a white bed. The woman looks up: "So many roses."

In the impenetrable afternoon.

She gives it up—that she was ever anything like, anything remotely like that dazzling young poet in a red dress. In the forest-fire region.

She tries to remember a poem. Out loud.

If you came back now and said—

I would say: I forgive you. Come back. And that would be a lie.

And in the night under the strangled, white lights if you tried to say . . . to explain. I would say: OK, OK, and we would think we were safe.

She dares not touch the luminous fur of the cat. She sees the red drinks and polka dots. The boats. Each object not so terribly alone, she supposes.

"Strange one," they all say. "She brings upon herself the end."

We walked in tall grass and were alive.

He's standing at the fountain. She walks through the agony of the afternoon. She's weaving a little bit. Sometimes the Chinese hat does not seem like much protection. He comes forward. She stops. Just stands there.

You take your places. You bow your lovely heads deeply. Step into this last pose. You prepare to enter the room one last time together. L'innocence des fleurs.

"How much you are like a photograph now." He takes her big boxy camera and aims it at her.

"Dit fromage," he says.

"Non."

"Dit non à la drogue."

"Non."

"Dit au revoir."

"Non." Though this is good-bye.

"Dit rien."

She says nothing now.

## 27

They sit in the white room beyond despair. Where they watch and are watched.

I see the two in the passive afternoon, stripping each other of everything. Laughing slightly. Whispering. They were lovers once.

"Look, Lucien, how alike they have become. If you looked at them from across the square it would be almost impossible to tell them apart. They have become the same thing," she says.

Could she ever have loved him, she wonders?

"I thought you said it never rained in summer."

He can't bear her saying this anymore. He leads her to the bed.

I smile. They were lovers once.

He wants her to stay here in the white room with him. He says it in English: "Stay. The light of September . . . and the fountain—once the tourists have gone."

He holds her down, delicately pinning the wings of the angel, the butterfly. She lies motionless on the bed. He has never seen her as beautiful as she is now. He closes his eyes and sees swans. Swans where there were none. Girls by the fountain.

He could almost believe those swans were everything worth living for.

"Tu es belle," he says.

She smiles. "Non." She wonders why everything arrives

too late.

"Cheveux longs," she says.

They imagine roses swollen with rain. Floating in their watery globes. She trembles. Outlines where she imagines his heart to be, floating. . . .

He sighs.

He seems suddenly small to her and she is afraid. She touches his face and wonders how she could have ever thought it meant forever. He is speaking softly, in a language she does not know. In a gentle voice.

Words say: rain. Late.

Words say: stay.

But they've lost their power now.

Her notebook gone. Gone the hunger for figs. The hunger for an arrangement of anything.

The black book falls. And she is just a woman in a white room, that's all. It doesn't mean anything. She can't remember what it means.

She opens her legs. She laughs at the savage and dazzling center she thought once might save her. She pets the small torture of hair. Where she once thought: love, or oblivion in the swollen afternoon—or forever . . . Heaven.

She lights a terrible match. "I am Joan of Arc." He takes her arm. "Non!" He says: "Sacré," and "ça c'est sacré." Doesn't he see the charred and ruined eye? He takes her arm: "Non. Stop." Doesn't he see the blind eye? In the agony of her body she lights a terrible match.

"Non! Tell me a story," he begs.

In the savage and beautiful afternoon they practiced honte and au revoir. Rien and fin.

"Once upon a time," she says miserably.

"Oui?"

She doesn't know what else to say. "That's all. C'est tout."

He tells her there were books she wanted to write.

"Tell me about the young arlésienne," he says.

She smiles. "The Place du Docteur Pomme," she says. "She went to get well." She can't remember much of it.

Maybe he is inside her now. She can't be sure. The body a last vague—

He whispers, "Tell me about the poet in the red dress."

I see his face smile. The pulsing rose of his heart.

"Les Galeries Lafayette," he says. She shrugs. She can't remember the beginning, or the end. "Yes, there was an enormous city," she says. "There was a woman once."

She wonders why it was she always cried.

"You saw swans," he says.

"I saw a red horse."

"Tell me," he says, "about the French man by the fountain."

"What French man?"

"You said he was Franz Liszt in another life."

She laughs. "No, you must be mistaken." She shakes her head no.

Love is what is dangerous, Lucien. Careful.

"He was going to sail in a boat. Change the names of the world."

"Yes, she gave him hope. He was still quite young then."

"Oui. You said it." He is speaking very loudly, as though she is deaf now. "He met a mermaid. She had three waves in her hair. She said, 'Je t'adore.'"

"Yes, that's 'I adore you' in another language."

"You said he was from a film of Truffaut."

She smiles, pets his hand. Drifts in a dead language. With wires in her head.

"No. I don't remember."

She is tired now. "They were only stories," she says. "They didn't mean much."

"He works at the galerie that faces the fountain. The man with the cheveux longs. You said: swans."

"Are you sure?"

He holds her feathered neck in his hands. "Stay here," he says. He seems to be shouting. Everything magnified. My older brother waving and waving. So small. "Reste ici avec moi." He wraps his hand tighter around her neck in the raging afternoon. "I thought you said love."

"Don't let her get away," I whisper. "Look how easily she could escape."

He just wants to hear about the French man once more. The fountain.

"Help her," I beg. "She does not feel at home here."

He nods.

The full moon hurts them. Their one-eyed albino hope.

"Reste ici," he says. "Stay. Je t'aime."

She smiles. Everything arrives too late.

What have they understood? French people pass. Talking.

He holds her neck. Tighter. More tightly. She puts her hand over his in the catastrophic room. In the red room. "A little harder now," she says. "Un peu plus."

"Dépêche-toi. Harder," she begs.

"You said love."

So much silence. She can barely breathe. More. She sees his face smile.

Her breath almost gone.

"Reste ici," he says, and weeps.

### 28

The light. The light of septembre. Of September.

The light of septembre is la plus belle, he says. And he is right. The red wrung, the red wrung neck has turned black. Like a swan. She wears the black crown gracefully now. She walks to the fountain in silence.

He is no longer there.

She hears a high sound. Like mermaids or birds. She's watching her hat. Strange angel. Butterfly.

"Where is the man who always stood here? The man with the cheveux longs?"

"La côte basque," says the patron.

She smiles. "The most beautiful coast in the world."

"He never fit in here," the patron says. "He was never really a part of things."

"Oui, c'est vrai," she says.

"He was always a stranger here."

"Yes. I remember."

"He has gone home. To Biarritz."

She laughs. Maybe there is some hope for him.

No one knows why this cannot be. But it cannot.

I see now that it is going to take a great deal to wipe the glass eye bright. "Sorry," she whispers.

She waves to someone in a white bed. He is dying.

"So much silence maintenant." In the dazzling.

She runs her hands under the water of the midget sink of the Bar Internationale in the unbearable heat.

I think her story is almost over now. She is not so frightened anymore by the figs or the light. The forever.

I see her Chinese hat has tipped back. She wanted to be a bird, but she never could.

I think you were very lovely that day with your wings, opening the shutters.

This is her walk. Her very red walk.

People were laughing. People were talking. Singing the words.

She reaches. Reaches for the knife. She thinks she should be more afraid at this moment, but she is not. One should feel something more.

How small she is suddenly. And her small offrandes. Love. All those lights were people's lives.

She watches her veins open—a cathedral of light. Her blood rings like bells. Confetti. Angel. Stranger.

She waves. Wavers. In the agony of the afternoon. In a red dress.

Close your eyes now. Row your boat. Row your small boat.

Everyone here is kissing. And I am getting—I am getting dazzling now—dizzy now—too.

She steps into the fountain in the dazzling silence. Wipes her face with her flaring wrists and looks out on a world on fire.

It's not like we didn't try . . .

The light of September is the most beautiful.

A high sound like burning. . . . Stranger. Light. The sound of water over stones. She waves. Each word in its watery globe. Pulses. Once, twice, good-bye: *Love. Forever.* A woman. Floating like a heart. And roses.

# Acknowledgments

Je t'embrasse:

Chantal Akerman, Roland Barthes, Samuel Beckett, Maurice
Blanchot, Marguerite Duras, Johann Wolfgang von Goethe,
Friedrich Hölderlin, Julia Kristeva, Clarice Lispector,
Stéphane Mallarmé, Thomas Mann, Alain Resnais, Alain
Robbe-Grillet, James Salter, Nathalie Sarraute, Claude Simon,
François Truffaut, Paul Valéry, Edmund White.


Merci mille fois:

Judith Karolyi, Zenka Bartek, Ilene Sunshine, Robin Becker,
Sally Greenberg, Laura Mullen, Jojo Riva, Russell Beedles,
Pascal Paradis, Didier Bonnet, Louis Asekoff, Nancy Honiker,
Jeffrey De Shell, Lisa Springer, Dixie Sheridan, John O'Brien,
Jason Shinder, Kenneth and Rosemarie Maso, Steven Moore,
Barbara Ras, and Barbara Page.